The Throne Eternal

A novel written by Matthew J Elliott

Based on the story by Darren G. Davis & Ali Russell

FIRST PRINTING, September 2018.
Harry Markos, Director.

Paperback: ISBN 978-1-912700-13-4
eBook: ISBN 978-1-912700-14-1

Book design by: Ian Sharman

Cover by Rove

www.markosia.com

First Edition

Dedicated to Edgar

PROLOGUE
3200 BC

The Eclipse was almost total. The moonlight alone, shining through the perfectly circular hole in the ceiling, was usually sufficient to light Set's temple. Tonight, he had his servants light the torches. Tonight, the alignment would be perfect, and Set did not wish a single moment of his father's demise to go unobserved. Equally, he did not wish Rah to fail to notice the bejewelled statues dedicated to his son as he met his end. In those final moments, as he lay struggling in the sarcophagus that lay open before the altar, the Sun God would be in no doubt as to who had robbed him of his existence.

It did not occur to Set that his plan might not succeed; of course it would. He had only one serious concern – that his father and his sister might not fully understand. This was not a question of right and wrong, of good and evil. This was about balance. And tonight, the balance would be tipped in his favor.

He took a moment to glance at the contents of the cauldron. The silvery liquid was boiling nicely. It offended Set's ego that he would have to keep watch on the cauldron himself – hardly a task for one of the mightiest beings in the world, but he could spare none of his servants for such a task. Even though he had imbued them with formidable strength, overpowering Rah would be no easy task. And he would need to ensure that his temple was guarded against intruders. One intruder, specifically. Ah, sister, he thought to himself, you've always been more trouble than you're worth. But no longer. No longer.

Set's head snapped round as he heard a familiar voice yelling, threatening, roaring with fury... everything, in fact, but begging for mercy. How typical of father, he considered. And yet, how proper. Anything else would have been quite inappropriate.

The two largest of Set's slaves, their eyes glowing gold with his essence, emerged into the light, each grasping one of Rah's arms as he struggled to free himself. Set imagined that the others he had sent had not survived the initial battle with his mighty father. He had expected nothing else, and he would soon have no shortage of slaves, anyway. The loss was an entirely acceptable one.

"Unhand me at once, I command you!" Rah bellowed. He seemed incapable of doing anything quietly, but in his present situation, a display of rage was surely understandable.

A simple gesture from Set, and his burly servants forced Rah to his knees before his the altar. Of course, the mighty ruler must surely know who had done this to him, but there was an order to these things that must be observed. Slowly, Set lowered the hood of his robe, permitting his father to see him, to gaze into his green eyes. Now he would be certain. They gazed at one another for a full minute before Rah's head dropped, in either an admission of defeat or a declaration of disappointment.

"The urn..." Rah murmured. "it contains lead from the mines of Anubis, I imagine?" Set was surprised, not by the question, but by the fact that he had never heard his father say *anything* in a murmur before. "What unrighteous act have I committed, that my own son would wish a thousand deaths upon me?"

Set did not reply. Why make it too easy? He simply smiled and nodded to his men. They needed no detailed instruction, thanks to the total control he wielded. Once more, they grabbed their captive, and forced him up the steps of the altar.

Watching him struggle and complain, Set toyed with the idea of removing the crown from Rah's head before putting him to death. But, no. Let his humiliation be complete. Besides, he wanted no symbols of his father's reign.

The old man kicked and spat as they forced him into the sarcophagus. Set took a few steps back to avoid becoming involved in the unpleasantness. His father's robe was torn open, exposing his chest, specifically the area of his heart. Before Set was done, it would first be broken, then destroyed completely.

"Injustice, injustice!" wailed Rah as he was held down. "Your time shall come, Set! I will be avenged!"

Now, at last, the moment was right. As he reached for the lid of the sarcophagus, Set finally spoke, the last thing his father would ever hear, "Know that your daughter shall meet you in the underworld."

For the first and only time, Set observed fear on the old man's face. He said only one more word before the lid slammed shut.

"Isis..."

As his servants struggled with the urn, their master slowly opened a slat in the lid, positioned directly over the occupant's heart. Set allowed himself a full grin as he watched the sarcophagus rattle violently. But there was no way out for Rah, no way that led back to this world. The screams Set heard as the liquid lead was poured through the slat seemed to him sweeter than wine. As the moon covered the sun completely, the struggling ceased.

But the moment of satisfaction did not last. Out of the corner of his eye, he was aware of some disturbance near the entrance to the chamber. A flash of fiery red told him all he needed to know – it emanated from the gems on a gold bracelet identical to that worn by Rah himself.

So soon, he thought.

The massive guard he had placed at the entrance hurtled through the air and came to land at Set's feet. How gratifying to think that he would be able to keep his promise to his late father so soon.

The mere sight of Isis, impossibly tall and unfathomably beautiful, would have stunned any mortal man. But Set was not impressed by her appearance or her raven black hair. Her jewel-encrusted armor provoked in him not awe but irritation, since it had been a gift from their father, and Rah was not noted for his generosity – certainly not where his son was concerned.

Set motioned to his other minions to dispose of her, but he had no confidence that they would detain her for long. He was right to be wary – both men were lying at her feet in a moment, the golden glow gone from their dead eyes.

"The fight is not yet over, brother."

There was only one response to such a challenge, and it promised to be almost as satisfying as what he had done to Rah. Set opened the sarcophagus so that Isis could observe the interior. The lead had done its work; Rah's body had vanished completely. But she could be in no doubt that the coffin had once contained their father's body, for his golden bracelet remained.

There were tears in his sister's eyes, as she choked back a sob. And yet there was no sadness in those eyes; rather, they burned with hatred.

"There is only one way to kill a God, Isis," Set told her as he slipped the bracelet onto his wrist.

"I am well aware of that." From the sheath at her hip, she drew a long curved knife, one that he had not seen before. Odd, he thought, where could she have come by it? There was something about the blade... No, she couldn't have been to the mines, too! Cunning little minx. Nothing for it now, but to brazen it out.

"Simply give me your bracelet, sister, and what must be shall be."

"You will have to cut it from my dead wrist," she replied, through gritted teeth.

"That would be most agreeable." Set shrugged off his robe. It would only be in the way in what was to come.

When Gods fight, it is at a supernatural speed. Were any whose minds had not already been infected by Set been watching, they would have found the battle almost impossible to follow. Isis and Set possessed an agility that laughed at the laws of physics.

Repeatedly, Isis swung her weapon, with the intention of piercing Set's skin. Repeatedly, he blocked her attacks with his recently procured bracelet, sending sparks flying in all directions. Brother and sister were equally matched, and neither would tire, but Set was aware that a lucky swing of the blade might bring his plans to a premature end. I can't waste any more time like this, he thought, as Isis came within a whisker of slicing his throat open. I need reinforcements.

The moon was moving off the sun, revealing half light, half darkness, as Isis made one final attempt to stab Set, but his reactions were too fast. Ducking her blade, he swung around, his elbow striking her in the gut and knocking her to the ground.

A scampering sound heralded the arrival of reinforcements – scorpions, scurrying into the temple. In that form, they would have presented an annoyance for Isis, but that was not her brother's intent. Before her eyes, the creatures grouped together, rapidly forming into human shapes – more of Set's minions with the glowing gold eyes. Isis braced herself, ready to leap up and defend herself. Too late. Several sets of powerful hands grabbed her limbs, pinning her down.

Set shot her a mischievous grin, as he reached down and plucked the knife from her hand.

"Thank-you, Sister. This should do nicely."

"I won't make it easy for you!"

"I would expect nothing else. But that predictability is your fatal weakness, just as it was Rah's."

As he spoke, Set angled the knife, intending to plunge it beneath her breastplate, directly into her heart. There it was. One good thrust should do it, and the reign of Set can begin in earnest. His shoulders stiffened as he readied himself.

That was his crucial error, for at that same moment, Isis, seeing that he was about to strike, flinched. There was no way of avoiding the blade, but it penetrated her shoulder not her heart. The scorpion-men relaxed their grip, allowing Isis to kick Set in the chest. He stumbled backwards, landing on the steps of the altar. Any pain he felt, however, was minor compared to the suffering of his opponent, who lay writhing on the floor, the knife still protruding from her shoulder. Isis let out a gasp as the power of the blade she had intended to use against Set robbed her of her youthful glow.

Within seconds, her skin stretched tight across her bones. Almost skeletal, Set noted. And that from nothing more than a shoulder wound. He watched with fascination as, with the last of her strength, Isis gradually extracted the knife, every inch seemingly causing her more agony than the last. Most satisfy-

He hadn't even seen Isis hurl the knife that was now lodged in his stomach. He reached out to remove it, but his hands... His hands were shrivelling before him. His whole body...

A piercing shriek filled the entire chamber as Set's minions crumbled to dust at the very moment their master expired.

Isis blew the powdery remains of one of her enemies from her face, taking a final moment to appreciate the absurdity of the situation. She glanced across at the remains of her brother.

"Well," she whispered, "it appears we shall meet again."

When the high priests visited the temple the following day, they would find two skeletons, and every indication that a titanic struggle had taken place.

CHAPTER ONE
PRESENT DAY

Breath control. That was the secret.

Some days, Bruce Stone thought he should have been an actor instead of an archaeologist. Too much of his time was spent this way, auditioning from the trustees and professors of Colombia University. Trying to put a positive spin on grave-digging. Pleading for funding.

He was too damn proud, that was the problem. Each refusal stung his ego. He couldn't eat for days before each new presentation.

He was glad Alex couldn't see him. What would she think of her dad now? He prided himself on remaining composed, secretly pleased that she could her boast to her friends of having a "cool" parent. Assuming she had friends. He chewed his lip, as he tried to access that portion of his memory. Of course Alex had friends. She must have, she's seventeen, for God's sake. Didn't he remember her saying something about a "Sharon"? No, not Sharon. Shannon, that was it. See, I knew she had friends, he told himself. A responsible parent knows what's going on in his kid's life, but he keeps a respectful distance. Now stop distracting yourself, and focus.

In the absence of a mirror, he checked his hairline with his fingertips, ensuring there were no rogue strands. He wasn't, he believed, particularly vain, but he was quietly pleased with what his daughter described as his "Jon Stewart do": sufficient gray to suggest authority, but not so much that it appeared he might start drooling into his cereal any day now.

He heard coughing from the assembled academics. They were getting restless, expecting something special from him. Luckily, he could barely see them. The only light in the boardroom came from a projector, operated by his assistant, Simon. Which puts me in the spotlight, Bruce considered. Think of it this way: at least you can't see their expressions while they watch you screw up. That sounded like the sort of thing Alex might say. How did she wind up with such a negative outlook, anyway? Hadn't he always tried to- Now, stop that! This parental control is commendable, he told himself, but this doesn't concern Alex. This is about Isis.

Taking one final moment to compose himself, Bruce checked his clothing for food stains, and strode fearlessly into the light.

This is it. Don't let them see fear. And control your breathing.

A nod to Simon was all that was required to instruct the young man to insert the first slide, a carved depiction of two Egyptian Gods, male and female. They'd briefly discussed the possibility of using computer graphics, Simon had even wanted to hand out 3-D glasses, but Bruce had been concerned that it would give the impression that they already had money to burn. No, he'd said, keep it low-tech.

He reached into his jacket pocket for his laser pointer. He felt a surge of panic as he realised that the last time he'd seen it was on the side of his plate in the university cafeteria as he looked for change. Well, he considered, it doesn't get much more low-tech than pointing.

"The, uh..." *Raise your voice, dummy!* "The figure on the left is Isis, the goddess of light and ruler of Egypt. On the right, is her brother, Set, the dark god of chaos."

So far, so good. Nobody was hearing anything they didn't already know, but nobody had walked out in disgust this time. He could never completely blot out the memory of that disastrous symposium at the Plaza Hotel in New York.

Bruce signalled Simon to change slides. Another representation of Set and Isis appeared on the screen behind him, this time engaged in a battle, weapons drawn.

"They were born of the sun god, Rah," Bruce went on. "Throughout history, Set was jealous that his sister was given reign of Egypt, and hatred towards Rah burned within him."

He took a moment to wipe a speck from his glasses leaving behind a large greasy smear. Damn cafeteria food. Something was burning within him, too; probably that burrito.

Without having to give the instruction, another slide was projected: Set standing at an altar.

"Set, uh... Well, he finally grew powerful enough among the high priests to exact revenge on his father. A murder so heinous, it would become legendary."

"'Mythological', not 'legendary'," he heard someone mutter to a colleague. "'Legendary' suggests a basis in fact."

Oh crap, he was losing them. "Set killed his father the only way it was possible to kill a..." he gulped, "...god. With molten lead from the mines of Anubis. But Set's sister Isis had visited the same mines, and fashioned the Knife of Horus to put an end to Set. They battled in Set's temple but the fight ended in a stalemate, with them both killing each other... somehow."

The lights came on at that moment, temporarily blinding Bruce and thus making it impossible to identify the board member who muttered, "Sounds more like an extravagant fairytale to me..."

Time to cut to the chase, Bruce realised. "The point is, I believe that the bodies of Isis and Set were moved from Set's temple and that their final resting place is in the so-called 'Tomb of the Gods' which is located underneath the Great Pyramid. I... have a slide..."

"I think we all know what the Great Pyramid looks like." Bruce recognised the voice of the mutterer, a short, balding man with gold-rimmed glasses. His name might be Houck. Then again, it might not. "And tell me, Dr Stone, what makes you think Egyptians would dig up the graves of their gods?"

"Isis and Set's mortal bodies were believed to have been entombed in ornate gold sarcophagi," he responded, undeterred. "Any pharaoh would want to be surrounded by such wealth upon entering the afterlife. I'd say that a god and goddess rate a holy tomb, wouldn't you?"

If he'd expected anyone to nod in agreement, he was doomed to disappointment.

"Giza has been heavily excavated, and yet no-one has discovered your 'Tomb of the Gods', Doctor. How do you account for that?" his heckler enquired.

"I'm fully aware of the number of digs at that locale, but I have substantial evidence that the site is the centre for godly worship, especially Isian."

"Impressive, Dr Stone..."

All the heads of the seated board members snapped round at the sound of the heavily accented-voice. Bruce recognised the speaker as Ahmed.

Shaven-headed and built like a former professional wrestler, it was hard to imagine what influence he held over the academics. Or it would have been, were it not for the gold jewellery encircling his throat, wrists and fingers. There's more where this came from, it seemed to say. A lot more.

"But all Egyptians," Ahmed continued, "and all archaeologists know that the Great Pyramid was constructed for the Pharaoh Khufu."

"Then I'm sure all Egyptians will also recall the 'Inventory Stela', which concedes that the pyramid was actually a temple dedicated to Isis."

Ahmed strode purposefully toward Bruce, who tried not to wince at the sight of the Egyptian's horribly crooked nose.

"I have seen the markings you refer to, Doctor. Those markings are from the twenty-first Dynasty, surely."

"I disagree. I believe they are the genuine form of the fourth Dynasty." Bruce hoped he sounded confident. He was all too aware that Ahmed was sizing him up, while the audience waited intently for one of them to snap, preferably Bruce.

At last, the Egyptian said, "You had better be right," and stalked back to where Dr Williams, president of the board, was seated.

Bruce noticed Simon mouth the words, "What the hell was that?" In return, he could only shake his head in bemusement. What was Ahmed saying? Was he telling Williams he wanted Bruce fired? Or maybe locked in a crate and dropped in the ocean? There was no doubt he possessed the wealth and influence required to do either. Or both.

After what seemed like half an eternity, Dr Williams rose.

"Dr Stone," she began, "on behalf of the board, I'd like to say..."

Pause. Bruce wanted to scream, what? What? This isn't *American Idol*, just tell me!

"...pack your bags for Egypt!"

The relief was so great; Bruce was astonished to discover just how tense he had been. Right now, he felt like a puppet whose strings had just been cut. He wanted to throw his hands into the air triumphantly, but he no longer had the strength. It was just as well he hadn't acted in such a congratulatory fashion, as just then, Dr William's features took on the unpleasant aspect displayed by Ahmed a moment earlier.

"But remember this, Doctor," she advised him, "you better find something."

In an instant, his smile evaporated.

CHAPTER TWO

"Two weeks, that's firm."

Bruce doubted that Dr Williams could see his startled expression as she stalked through the corridor ahead of him. Damn, she was fast. Was she one of those speed-walkers?

"Two weeks?" he repeated. "There's just no way my crew will be able to dig that fast!"

"They'll have to. Two weeks, Bruce. And you only got the second week because Mr Ahmed has been so generous as to partially finance this excavation."

He felt like dropping to his knees right there and crying "Why?" to the heavens, but instead he just emitted a growl of frustration.

Dr Williams stopped in mid-stride and turned round. Bruce almost didn't notice, and narrowly avoided colliding with her.

"Why? You just told a roomful of professors you wanted to search for the bodies of two gods. Gods, Bruce. And you don't think that would give anybody pause?"

"Well, not gods *per se*, but-"

"Look, Bruce," she said in a sympathetic tone he didn't believe for a moment, "We've all been very understanding of your recent loss, but... it's been a year."

Wow, he thought, a whole year. Imagine that. Wasn't there a line in *Hamlet* about that?

"We're losing money on your digs, Bruce." She gave him a pat on the shoulder he couldn't help but find unsettling. "You have to deliver this time. Let's face it. You aren't what you used to be."

No, I used to be a husband and a father, he mused as Williams marched away from him. Now Marie is gone, and I'm just a father. For the second time in just a few hours, he was glad Alex couldn't see him. Has anyone ever been so pathetic?

***

The same question ran through Alex Stone's mind just a few hours earlier, as she sat terrified on the bed, her knees touching her chin.

Pictures of some of the world's most exciting and exotic locations decorated the walls of her dorm room, most of them newspaper clippings regarding her parents' archaeological discoveries. In the time her mom and dad were together, they must have faced unimaginable dangers. But their only kid couldn't get off her bed because there was a spider on the carpet. Okay, it wasn't just any spider; it was a humongous spider, just standing there, terrifyingly still.

Wasn't it supposed to be the case that as she got older, things would look smaller? Like, one day, she'd return to Northwood Boarding School and gasp, "Wow, everything looks so tiny!" adding,

"Why, yes, I believe I am the first Olympic athlete-slash-supermodel ever to win the Nobel Prize for Chemistry, thank-you for asking." So why the hell did spiders seem a lot bigger to her at seventeen than they had when she was just a kid? She was pretty sure they weren't so mean-looking back then, either. This one was as big as her hand, and she could even see those things at the front, what do you call them? Pincers? Mandibles, something like that? It didn't really matter, she could see them and it freaked her the hell out. In the past, Shannon had tried to convince her that spiders in the States were all harmless. If that was true, what did they need those pincer/mandible things for? She'd never confessed it to anyone, not even Shannon, but she couldn't even watch the first Spider-Man movie from the beginning, for fear of seeing Tobey Maguire getting bitten. She usually started from the scene where he wakes up totally cut.

I am going to be so late, Alex told herself. And what am I supposed to say? Sorry I missed half the lesson, Mr Willowby, there was an incident. What kind of incident? Well, it involved a spider. No, not just any spider, I'm pretty sure it was one of those Australian redback spiders, the ones that live in toilets and like to bite people on the ass with their pincers. Or possibly their mandibles. Yeah, that's totally a real thing. We've all heard stories, right?

Alex glanced at the framed picture of her mother on her nightstand.

"Sorry, Mom. I don't know how to be fearless like you."

Her eyes returned to the spider. She was pretty sure it was closer now. She hadn't seen it move an inch since she first spotted it, but that just made it more frightening, the belief that it might at any moment leap through the air and attach itself to her face.

The spider continued to do nothing, in that defiant way she'd become familiar with during the last half hour. Her shoes were on the floor, within arm's length. The question was, could she reach one before it attacked, infecting her body with a cocktail of toxins, each one more fatal than the last? No more thinking, Alex, this is the time for action – now. OK, now. Right now. The next "now" will definitely be it. Now. Count of three, maybe?

With a cry of, "Up yours, Charlotte!" Alex grabbed a brown oxford and slammed it down on her foe, sending it to Spider Hell. Victory. Oh, God, she hoped it didn't have babies.

In the corridors, a bell rang.

"No, no, no, no!" She wasn't ready, not even close! She turned and headed for the bathroom, instantly tripping over her backpack. Ow. Setting the bag upright again, she held the door frame to help her get back on her feet. Sure that was undignified, she admitted to herself, but at least take comfort in the fact that there wasn't anyone else around when you made yourself look like a total- Oh no, not again.

Some time during the night, it seemed that a small, controlled explosion had occurred in her hair. Now it seemed to be trying to make a break for it, heading in all possible directions simultaneously. At least when Anne Hathaway looked this lame in *The Princess Diaries*, it turned out that underneath she was, well, Anne Hathaway. Alex was resigned to the fact that she would never turn out to be Anne Hathaway underneath – not even Anne Hathaway in *Bride Wars*, which pretty much sucked. Where the hell was the brush? How did this keep happening to her? She tried to be organized, she really did, but stuff just disappeared. Her Grandmother had copied out a prayer to Saint Anthony, the patron saint of lost items, instructing her to say it at times like this. The piece of paper with the prayer on it had gone missing almost immediately. She'd never had the heart to tell Grandma.

With a deep sigh, she resorted to running her hand under the faucet and hoping that her wet fingers would untangle the mess. No such luck. Her hand actually got stuck in there, and when she eventually managed to wrench it free, several strands of hair came with it. Realising she couldn't waste any more time on this hopeless cause, Alex flew out of the bathroom, tripping over her backpack once again, her right knee landing with a squelch in the remains of a squashed spider.

It's just a phase, she thought as she grabbed a pile of books. I mean, I can't live forever. I just have to keep remembering that after today, I'll be away from this living hell for a few weeks... and probably counting down the days until I have to come back to this living hell. Hopefully, Grandma was wrong when she said that these were the best years of my life; if that's true, then I've been royally screwed.

***

It seemed to Alex as she dashed through the quad that her fellow students must operate on an entirely different timescale. How could they just *walk* from one place to another? Were minutes and seconds longer for everyone else? Nikki and Ellen never seemed to be in a hurry to get anywhere. They just ambled along, casually dribbling a football as they went. Somehow, they just seemed to know that whatever was at their destination, it wouldn't start until they got there. Was it because they were soccer captains, or was it mostly the boobs? Mostly the boobs, she decided.

At her present rate of speed – calculated to get her to Mr Willowby's class not-quite-in-time – Alex completely failed to notice the conspiratorial smile shared by Nikki and Ellen. Nor did she see Ellen stop the soccer ball under her heel before kicking it as hard as she could in the direction of a fast-moving target, easily identifiable by the disaster that passed for a hairstyle.

Alex was wondering what all the students in the quad were watching with anticipation before being struck on the back of the head by a football, which knocked her to the ground and caused her to let go of her books, sending them scattering in all directions. She saw that skin had been scraped from her palms before she realised just how much it hurt. But by far the worst thing about such a public humiliation was the fact that expressing any discomfort only made it worse. Bad enough that everyone was laughing at you, why add to your humiliation? She noticed that Nikki and Ellen didn't even bother to pretend that it was an accident – not even so much as an insincere "oops".

"Nice head-butt, Frizzball!" yelled Nikki before strutting off after her ally.

"This is nothing like *Mean Girls*," Alex muttered to herself, as she began picking up her books and dusting them off.

"Alex, are you alright?" Alex didn't have to look up to know who it was; only Shannon O'Leary would be concerned enough to enquire about her well-being.

"I'm fine, actually," Alex lied. "It's cool. This is only the third time today I've been knocked on my ass – that's a pretty good average for me."

"Bella Swan was pretty clumsy, too," Shannon pointed out.

"Yeah, but she had a lot of other issues, too. Plus, she was fictional. I don't really see myself spending my immediate future choosing between dating a vampire or a werewolf. I'm going to be too busy getting kicked in the head by Ellen and Nikki."

"Yeah, I saw them high-fiving after they got you," Shannon informed her, handing her the remainder of her badly-scarred textbooks.

"I didn't. I was too busy checking out the floor. I've seen so much of it, I could probably specialize."

"You know they only treat you like this because they're jealous."

"Yeah, all this and brains, too."

"I'm serious, Alex. With their brains combined, they're still not as smart as you. Maybe they think by hitting you in the head with soccer balls, they can kill some of your brain cells, so you'll be dumb enough to talk to them." Shannon laughed so hard at her own joke, her glasses began to slip down her nose.

"Right now I don't care about brain cells, Shannon, I care about these!" She motioned to the area where, typically, one would expect to find a pair of teenage breasts. "You've seen Nikki's, right? How do they stay up in the air like that? Hasn't she ever heard of Newton?"

"Of course not." her friend responded.

"I guess not."

"You know they'll be down to her ankles when she's sixty."

"Great, so I just have to bide my time."

"You really think all Chris is interested in is big tits?"

"Is he seventeen years old?"

"OK, I withdraw the question. Come on, Alex, we're gonna be late for class. I mean, more so than usual."

Really, thank God for Shannon, thought Alex as they made their way to Mr Willowby's history lesson. She's pretty enough not to have to hang around with me. Maybe not pretty enough to hang around with Nikki and Ellen, but she could still get a better class of friend if she wanted. She always said the right thing at times like this, and she never asked embarrassing or awkward questions.

"So what's up with your hair?" asked Shannon, exploding Alex's mental picture of her.

"It tried to eat my hand. I got it back after a life-or-death struggle."

"Didn't have time to brush it?"

"For all I know, the brush is probably in there somewhere. It looks pretty bad, huh?"

"It can still be saved, Alex. Maybe if I use my fingers- Oh my God, it's carnivorous!"

"Don't struggle, it can sense fear. Ouch! I said don't- Owww!"

And so it went on, all the way to history class...

CHAPTER THREE

...which proved to be as big as disaster as Alex had anticipated. She was stupid to think that Chris's decision to pick the seat next to hers was based on anything other than lack of availability. God, he was gorgeous: sandy blonde hair, baby-blue eyes, dazzling smile. Did he know what he did to her? More importantly, did he care? Probably not. She just had to make him care. There were magazines that gave tips on stuff like that, but Alex had always considered herself above buying that trash. Right now, as he flicked an unruly strand of hair from his face – God, even his forehead was sexy! - she would've traded every page of *Anna Karenina* for just one piece of advice that worked. Her Grandmother often said: "Faint heart never won fair maiden," which wasn't especially useful, since Alex wasn't interested in maidens. But she got the point. She had to be fearless.

"Hi... Alex..." she said in a less than fearless manner. But at least she got it out. Stage One complete. If he responded, she could move on to Stage Two. First, though, she would have to *think* of a Stage Two.

But it didn't matter. Chris had already turned away from her, speaking to Nikki, who, along with Ellen (naturally!) was seated behind them.

Bitch, Alex though, before chiding herself for being unfair. Then it occurred to her that this was Nikki she was thinking about, and that it was totally fair. She reinstated the "bitch".

"Hey, Nikki, you got an extra pen?" Chris asked, in that way he had.

Smiling, Nikki shook her head. She held up a pink pen with a flower at the top. "Sorry. My only one."

My time to shine, Alex thought proudly.

Chris turned back to find a pen just inches from his nose.

"Here," Alex announced, and her tone was much more determined. She was offering him her only pen, true, but damn it was worth it for the look that passed between them. It was electric (on her side, anyhow). How could he miss the longing in her gaze?

"Thanks," he said, before whipping around and handing the pen to Ellen.

"Okay, so what's your number?"

And Alex just had to sit there while Ellen wrote her cell number down with Alex's pen! Right now, the idea of a hole opening up and swallowing her seemed incredibly attractive. Was she turning red? She felt hot, so she was pretty sure she was turning red.

Shannon, who might not have possessed enough tact not to mention her hair, at least knew that now was not the time for words. She simply handed Alex a spare pen, and life carried on sucking, as it usually did.

The results of the last exam gave her no real pleasure, even though her grade was pretty much a foregone conclusion. Hey, if the daughter of not one but two archaeologists couldn't ace a history test, what was she good for? Attracting the ruggedly handsome captain of the Lacrosse team? Some hope of that.

Chris, the ruggedly handsome captain of the Lacrosse team, simply gave an insolent shrug as Mr Willowby placed a piece of paper bearing a C- in front of him.

"Come on, Chris," Willowby said, before turning and delivering Nikki's exam... a D. No surprise there, and even less of a shocker that she didn't seem to care in the slightest.

"Nikki, I expected more from you," Willowby told her. Considering Nikki's general conduct in class, Alex figured that couldn't possibly be true.

"The bleach starting to seep in, Nikki?" Shannon taunted. "Sizzle, 'bye now. I should totally do stand-up."

Nikki shot her a peevish glance and looked away.

Upon discovering that she'd gotten a B+, Shannon nodded approvingly.

Last, but not least, Alex.

"I'd like to acknowledge the only student ever to receive a 100% on my final exam... Miss Stone."

It was a hollow victory, of course. She shrank down into her seat, as she became the target of mocking laughter from the other kids. There was no glory in academic excellence.

"Well done, Alex." The fact that Willowby was looking down at her so proudly only seemed to make matters worse. Why couldn't he just go back to his desk? When would the agony be over?

"Alright, now that the school year has finally come to an end, let's hear what you kids are doing this summer."

Not this, she thought.

Ellen raised her hand, and what little attention had been focussed on Alex now evaporated.

"Yes, Ellen?"

"I'm vaycaying in the Hamptons with Nikki and her family." The air-headed friends beamed at each other.

Mr Willowby nodded slowly. "And I'm sure that will be...memorable."

"*Vaycaying*?" Shannon whispered. "Was a new word invented and someone forgot to notify me?"

"Shannon, what about you?" Willowby had obviously heard her.

"Oh, I'm backpacking through Europe with my parents and brother. *Half*-brother."

Mr Willowby raised his eyebrows. "Nice."

Without budging from his position in front of Alex, he gradually questioned the whole class about their plans: sailing camp in Canada, studying ballet at ABC in New York... Lacrosse practice, all summer for Chris, of course. As usual, Alex found it next to impossible to picture him with his shirt on.

"And what about you, Alex?"

She cringed.

"Who cares?" jeered Nikki.

"Probably studying on how to ace next year's final!" Ellen added.

Mr Willowby looked at Ellen, puzzled. "I don't get it."

While his attention was elsewhere, someone took the opportunity to throw a paper-ball at Alex's head, much to the enjoyment of her fellow class-mates. To make matters worse, instead of falling to the floor, it just got lodged in there. Not long now, she told herself. You just have to survive the rest of the day, and you'll be back where you belong.

***

Alex had never really had a problem with wearing a uniform, so hanging around in the Northwood School parking lot in her own clothes didn't feel like as much of a release to her as it did to others. Besides, what were they all doing but swapping one uniform for another? Was there a single student who hadn't chosen to express their individuality by wearing a t-shirt and ripped jeans? The only difference being that most people wore their jeans a lot tighter about the ass than she did. Alex didn't want either students or faculty to have to confront the unpalatable truth about the size and shape of her ass. Besides, she could never understand the attraction of asses, anyway. Except for Chris's ass, of course. Chris's ass was hypnotic. It seemed to follow her around the room. Or maybe she followed *it* around the room. She began to feel herself being swept away by her favourite daydream, the one where she took a wrong turn after gym, and found herself in the wrong showers... Actually, the fantasy was surprisingly chaste after that point. Alex wouldn't even admit it to her best friend, but she hadn't even kissed a boy yet; not that most of her classmates couldn't have figured it out for themselves.

"You need a ride to your grandma's again?" Shannon asked, dragging her back to cruel, unforgiving reality.

"Uh, no, my dad is picking me up."

Shannon raised an eyebrow at this news.

"Wow, the mysterious Dr Stone is finally surfacing, and I'm going to miss it!"

"Yeah, we have a few days here before the expedition in Giza starts, so I've planned some daddy-daughter stuff for us to do. Braid each other's hair, stuff like that."

Alex jumped as a panelled station wagon pulled up in front of them with a squeal of brakes that badly needed attention. She recognised the driving before the driver.

"There's my girls!" cried Shannon's mom as she kicked open the door, spilling candy wrappers all over the lot.

Alex gave her a feeble smile. "Hi, Janet."

"How are you, sweetie?" Alex couldn't shake the feeling that Janet called her "sweetie" only because she couldn't remember her actual name.

Shannon gave Alex a big hug. "Looks like I don't get to meet Indiana Jones after all," she sighed.

"He's not really anything like Harrison Ford, but he'll be glad you said it."

"Remember, sweetie, if you ever need anything, we're right here."

"In Europe," Alex noted as she watched Shannon wipe some more candy wrappers off the passenger seat and climb in next to her mom.

"That's right."

"Call me when you get back!" Shannon said, cheerily. "Have fun with your dad!"

"That goes for me, too," Janet added. "Have a great summer, Alice."

Shannon gave an enthusiastic wave, as Alex watched the car speed off, taking her best and only friend away.

Within half an hour, she was the last person still waiting to be picked up. An hour later, she was still waiting.

"WHERE R U?" She texted the same message five times. No reply.

Figures, she thought: if I'd been dead for centuries, Dad wouldn't wait a second before coming after me. But I'm alive, slumped against a trash can, and totally ignored. Wow, I'm actually envying the dead. By anyone's standards, that's got to be a cry for help.

CHAPTER FOUR

Alex spent most of the journey in her dad's SUV picking the nuts off the ice cream sundae he had presented her with as an apology.

"I am... so sorry Alex."

"Uh-huh." Can't believe he forgot about my allergies, she thought.

"There was a collision on the 91, and Boston was a nightmare. Hey, what happened to your jeans? Did you get into a fight?"

That, at least, merited a smile, she couldn't deny it.

"No, Dad, I bought them this way. They're distressed."

"Distressed?"

"Uh-huh."

He shook his head in confusion. "OK. And what's that thing on your knee? It looks like a squashed bug. If that's a tattoo, it better be a temporary, young lady."

At that moment, Alex felt so ridiculously happy, she actually thought she might cry. Her dad was right here, not on the other side of the world, and it didn't really matter that he disapproved of her; he was disapproving of her here, not via Skype, *here*.

She unzipped her backpack and pulled out her notebook.

"So, listen," she began, "according to CitySearch, the Webster Cliff's trail is amazing in the summer, and then Friday, I thought we could go into Bos...ton..."

Alex hadn't made it to the end of the sentence before she knew from her father's expression that they weren't going to do any of those things.

"Listen Alex, I am really, truly sorry-"

"But?"

"But I'm afraid I have to leave for Cairo sooner than I thought. We weren't granted as much dig time as I'd planned for, so the process has been sped up."

For Alex, it seemed like the perfect end to a perfect day. "You said you have to leave sooner. How soon is sooner?"

Bruce took a deep breath, readying himself for her reaction. "Tonight."

She didn't respond. Offering him the opportunity to dig a bigger hole for himself. Well, he's an archaeologist, she thought – that was what he's best at.

"It is imperative that I arrive in Giza by tomorrow evening. I'm bringing you to your grandmother's right now."

OK, that was deep enough. Time for an explosion. "*What the hell, Dad?*"

"Alex, I will not tolerate that kind of language. I am your father."

"Really? Well you sure don't act like it!"

Had she crossed a line? He looked hurt. Like she'd touched a really sore spot, and now he just wasn't able to speak. Screw it, she decided. She'd been hurt, too.

"So why did you even bother picking me up, Dad? And by 'picking me up', I mean 'picking me up *eventually*'? Why not just let Grandma do it?"

"Because believe it or not, I wanted to see you."

"I don't believe it, and you want to know why?"

"Sure."

"Because ever since Mom died, you've tried to act like I don't exist. Well I do, Dad. I'm right here!" She waved her arms around furiously, indicating the amount of space she took up. In her anger, she overdid it, causing her dad to swat her hand away when it began to obstruct his view.

"I am fully aware of your existence, Alex," he informed her in his best Dadly tones.

She shrugged. "OK, so I guess it's just that you don't like being around me."

"That's not true."

Nothing more was said for a few miles. Alex's ice cream had more or less melted without her even taking a taste. Drops were making a mess of the SUV's upholstery, and she didn't care one bit.

"You said you wanted me to join you in Giza? Well, I'm not going."

"Alex..."

"I'm not. You don't want me there anyways."

"That's not true. Of course I do. More than you know." His tone was not entirely convincing.

Upon their arrival at the family's Hampton home, Alex didn't even give him the opportunity to shift the car into park before leaping out, and running into the outstretched arms of her grandmother. Of course, Grandma knew. Dad must have called her. He could have called Alex on her cell too, but, hey, why spoil the surprise?

"Oh, my baby." Grandma stroked Alex's hair, and somehow avoiding getting caught up in it. Just like in the fairy tales, she told herself: going to Grandma's house. And she was the perfect fairy tale grandma, with soft grey curls and sparkling blue eyes. Of course, in the fairy tale, Grandma got eaten by the big bad wolf. OK, you're over-thinking it again, Alex, she chided herself. Just give in to your misery and let it all out. The tears she didn't know had been waiting to flow since her mother's funeral came willingly now.

She didn't want to raise her head; right now, there was no place in the world she would rather be, especially not Giza. She heard Bruce get out of the car, and was aware that he hadn't approached them.

"Listen, I, uh... I'd love to stay..."

"No he wouldn't," she somehow managed to say, cruelly. Nobody ever tells you about the staggering amount of snot involved when you cry your heart out. Unable to cope with it anymore, and all too aware that she was ruining her grandmother's gorgeous natural wool sweater, she disengaged herself from the hug, and raced inside the house.

Sitting under the open window in her room, she heard them talking.

"You're losing her, Bruce."

"I know, Mom. But how do I get her back?"

"If you can find thousand year old artefacts, you can find your daughter. You just need to put as much energy into that as you do into your excavations."

"You're right. Of course you're right. I'll call you when I land."

Alex didn't bother to watch her father return to his SUV and drive away. She was steadily rearranging the photographs of her mother in date order, up to just a month before her death, when her grandmother appeared in the doorway bearing hot chocolate.

"She looks so happy, doesn't she? You know, when your father first brought her home, I wasn't sure I approved of her. I was wrong, of course. That happens sometimes."

"Not often. I really miss her."

Her grandma sat down on the bed. "I know, honey. We all do."

Alex looked up at her. "Do I have to go to Egypt?"

"You know, I really think you do."

CHAPTER FIVE

Struggling with a duffel bag that seemed determined to slide off her shoulder, and dragging her two-wheeled bag behind her, Alex had no idea where to go. She'd foolishly assumed that the signs at Cairo International Airport would be in English. Big mistake. Would she wind up as the first tourist who never even made it out of the airport? As if Americans overseas didn't have a bad enough rep.

As she made her way towards what she imagined must be the exit doors, a man brushed past her, knocking her duffel bag, and causing her to lose control of the two-wheeled bag. The bag fell, and Alex fell with it.

Even in Egypt, I suck, she thought, gloomily. And this time, I didn't even get hit by a soccer ball. And there's no Shannon here to offer me any help.

"You need some help?"

The voice was unmistakeably young, unmistakeably male, and unmistakeably foreign.

You never get a second chance to make a good first impression, so she could only hope that the owner of the concerned voice was nobody who might possibly know who she might be.

"Alex Stone?"

"Yes," she almost groaned. It was even worse than she'd feared. He *was* handsome. He was also tall and dark. A little skinny, maybe, but he was only offering her his hand, not his hand in marriage. Nice smile, though. A little goofy, but nice. With surprising strength, he lifted her to her feet.

"I am Fusani. I am to take you to Giza. May I carry your bags?"

Would he be offended if she said no? Would he be more offended if she said yes? Oh God, why hadn't she read a guidebook on the plane? Damn you, *Perks of Being a Wallflower*, you were just too engrossing.

All she managed to say was, "Uhhh..." Smooth.

Without waiting for a more coherent response, Fusani said, "I don't wish to hurry you, Miss Stone, but your father awaits your arrival."

"Right, right. So, Fusani, I guess he gave you a picture of me, right?"

The young Egyptian appeared bemused.

"I mean... so you'd be able to identify me."

"No."

"So how did you know that I was me? I- I mean, the 'me' that I am?" Her subconscious screamed at her to stop, and, for once, she obeyed. It was actually pretty obvious; she was the only Caucasian girl in sight.

"Shall we go, Miss Stone? I'm sure you don't want to be the first tourist never to make it out of the airport."

"No!" she laughed. "No, that'd be... stupid. Out of the airport. Sure. Absolutely. And you don't have to call me 'Miss Stone'. You can call me 'Alex'."

"And you can call me Fusani."

"I think I already did. So how old are you? If that's not a personal question."

"It is a very personal question, but one I don't mind answering; I'm seventeen."

"What a coincidence! I'm- I'm seventeen, too." This time, her subconscious remained silent, forcing her to talk relentlessly in a near-incomprehensible fashion. What the hell was the matter with her?

***

Alex had heard stories about people picking up another language just by being around the people who spoke it. If that were true, she reasoned, then she should have been fluent in Egyptian by the time they reached Fusani's muddied jeep. Maybe it worked better if you heard the language spoken at a reasonable pitch, instead of yelled by dozens of people at once. She'd always prided herself on her cosmopolitan outlook, but even she had to admit that, save for the constant honking of cars (which reminded her very much of her visits to New York) this was all pretty damn foreign to her.

As Fusani threw her luggage into the trunk, she finally plucked up the courage to ask him something that had been bothering her since her arrival. "So, listen, I was just wondering... Where's my dad? I mean, how come he didn't come to get me himself?"

Fusani's broad smile suggested that he didn't see any particular problem with this. "He is very busy with the excavation. Couldn't be pulled away at the moment."

She rolled her eyes. "Figures."

Oblivious to her tone, he said, "Your father, he is a great man. Yes?"

"Oh, yeah, super. One of the best. There's no way I'd trade him for Channing Tatum and a two-week vacation in Cancun." She stomped sulkily to the passenger door. It was stuck shut, and remained that way in spite of her attempts to commit acts of violence upon it.

"Um, Fusani? We've got a little problem here."

Fusani sauntered over with an expression that suggested it was just too damn hot to worry about anything and delivered two sharp kicks to the door, which promptly popped open.

"Are you kidding me?"

"You just have to know the right place. Now let's go."

Alex was still trying to figure him out as they whizzed through the insanely busy streets of Cairo, avoiding all manner of four-legged creatures pulling entire families in carts.

She'd been attempting to buckle her seatbelt since they'd set off, and was wondering whether it, too, required a couple of kicks in just the right place. Terrific – lousy transportation, no Dad, they'd come within inches of hitting an old woman in the middle of the street balancing a table on her head, and now some lousy music on a lousy radio. She'd tried to be culturally sensitive, but her patience was just about exhausted.

"Cool music," she observed in a sarcastic tone, and instantly regretted it.

Fusani looked at her, confused. "You don't like?"

She shrugged, noncommittally. Ah, the hell with it. Too late to back out now.

"Haven't you ever heard of MTV?" she asked.

"Music television, yes."

"Uh-huh. And you still listen to this?"

"This is my father's band."

She winced. Oh, crap. "Seriously?"

"No." Then, laughing, he changed the station. The Black Eyed Peas blared out from the speakers.

Alex had no choice but to laugh, too. She'd been had, but she deserved it. "I can't believe you! What? What is it?"

Fusani was pointing ahead of them. Pointing at... the Pyramids. The actual pyramids. They were no longer a photo in a book, or an image on a TV screen. They were right in front of her, and they were gigantic. There sheer immensity took her breath away. I just wished I could find the right word for it, she thought.

"Breath taking, aren't they, Alex?" asked Fusani.

Yeah, that'll work.

***

Bruce took a swig from his bottled water. It'd been too long since his last dig; he'd forgotten how many of these he got through in a day. He couldn't shake the feeling that each shovelful of earth was bringing him closer to the end of his career, rather than closer to the remains of Isis and Set. Already the first excavation had been abandoned and a new hole dug slightly to its left.

"Just keep telling yourself it's not an exact science," he muttered, turning the pages of his old journal. Keep it low-tech, he had advised Simon back in the States, little realising that the trustees felt exactly the same way. He was now reduced to logging coordinates in this book.

He couldn't remember when he had taken the photograph of Marie that fell from its pages onto his makeshift table. He stared at it, suddenly oblivious of the activity around him. She looked so well, so wonderful.

"Oh, Marie," he sighed, longingly. "I wish you were somehow here again. I could use your guidance."

"You're welcome to it," a familiar female replied.

Bruce almost gasped in surprise, until a McDonald's bag dropped into his lap.

"And *this*. Look what I discovered."

Bruce reached into the bag and pulled out a Big Mac. "Definitely a sign of civilization. Thanks, Rachel." He took a bite. "The best discovery all day."

"Uh-oh, that sounds discouraging."

Bruce looked up into his assistant's eyes. Was it his imagination, or did the blue bandanna she wore match them precisely? And what was that warm sensation he felt around the area of- He grimaced as he realised that the grease from the McDonald's bag had seeped out onto the front of his pants. Sensational.

"Still haven't found what you're looking for?" asked Rachel.

"Huh?"

"I said, haven't you found anything yet?"

"Well," Bruce replied, tossing the bag into the sand and swiftly crossing his legs, "when I checked our data with the Stela, I found that the map we've been referencing is off by two degrees."

"Oh, yeah? Let me see." She leaned in, studying the map. Bruce was never quite certain of the reason, but he always felt uncomfortable when she got that close to him. Not so uncomfortable, however, that he would ever dream of protesting. Had any other member of the team invaded his space in this fashion, he wouldn't have hesitated in telling them to back off. So why make an exception for Rachel? And why had he slammed the journal shut before she could catch a glimpse of Marie's picture? He wasn't thinking straight, that's all. Too much exercise of the higher brain functions. He should've gone into basketball, like his father had wanted.

"That's amazing, Bruce. Great work," she enthused, and he instantly felt slightly better about the whole situation. Weird. Or maybe, he considered, very far from weird. Maybe, in fact, perfectly natural. And his training as an archaeologist had taught him to follow the signs, however faint they might appear.

"Listen, Rachel..."

"Dad!"

Had Bruce been as adept at spotting the signs of human behaviour as he imagined, he would have detected the faint trace of a frown from Rachel as Alex made her appearance. But his attention at that moment was devoted entirely to his daughter. Having made such a mess of their parting in the States, there was no way he was going to blow their reunion here. He ran to her, ready to enfold her in his arms, lift her off her feet. They would laugh, maybe even a few tears – joyful ones, naturally – and then life could go on as it had done before. But something happened in those last few steps. Maybe it was something in her eyes, or something that wasn't in her eyes. What was missing? Whatever it was, it pretty much stopped him in his tracks, just as it stopped Alex, too. Awkwardness set in. After considering each other for a few seconds, they finally engaged in a stiff, emotionless hug.

"So... how was your flight?" Bruce asked, purely for the sake of saying anything at all.

"Long," she replied, and there the matter rested.

Unnoticed until that moment, Fusani dropped Alex's bags down in front of her father. "As promised, Doctor."

"Thank you, Fusani," Bruce said, warmly. Clapping his hands together in a meaningless nervous gesture, he addressed Alex. "So, how about a tour of the camp?"

She nodded. "Sure."

Bruce hesitantly put his arm awkwardly around Alex, and directed her towards his table where Rachel stood waiting. At the sight of her, his troubled expression vanished, only to reappear on Alex's face.

"I'm glad you're here, Alex," Bruce whispered.

"You are?" she asked, at full volume. Her response was not what he'd hoped for. Perhaps that was why, as they reached Rachel, Bruce found that he was suddenly unable to look either of them in the face.

"Alex, I'd like to introduce you to Rachel. She's my assistant on the dig."

Rachel extended a hand of welcome. "Pleased to meet you, Alex. I've heard a lot about you."

With obvious reluctance, Alex took the proffered hand. Bruce sensed that this was going to be a problem. In fact, he'd suspected it for some time.

Seemingly oblivious to any such tension, Fusani simply smiled. Does that kid even have a clue, Bruce wondered?

Hoping to cause a distraction, and put an end to an uncomfortable situation, he motioned for Alex to look over the map. "You're just in time, kid."

"Time for what?"

"Well, just recently, we found that-"

He was about to point to the site of the most recent excavation, but as Alex leaned in for a closer look; she accidentally knocked over the remains of her dad's bottled water. Within seconds, the ink on sections of the map began to run.

"Oh my God!" exclaimed Rachel.

Alex winced. "Dad, I'm so sorry!"

"It's alright, honey, we just, ah, need some towels. I hope... "

"Alex, perhaps there's one in your luggage?" Fusani suggested, not sounding particularly perturbed.

"Maybe..."

Bruce was unable to contain his anger any longer. "'Maybe'? You're not sure?"

"I don't always know where my towel is!" Alex protested.

Hurriedly, Rachel grabbed her own backpack. "I think I've got one in here."

"Good work, Rachel! Be quick!"

Unwilling to be beaten, Alex unzipped her duffel bag and reached into it.

"It's OK, Alex," her father told her. "Rachel's got it."

Not what she wanted to hear. "I can find it, I know I can!"

Rachel beat her to it, pulling a rag from her pack and handing it to Bruce.

"You must have other copies of this map?" Fusani asked.

"You'd think so, but no," Bruce replied irritably, as he began mopping the water up with great care. "The map itself is an artefact. It shouldn't even be out of the museum. I blame myself for this..."

He looked across at Alex, who was now running this way and that with items of underwear in her hands. A sudden wind had picked up the moment she opened her luggage, and now her clothes were strewn across the desert.

"Oh, for Christ's sake," he said to himself. None of his crew seemed inclined to assist her, and that damned Fusani simply stood there, laughing.

Satisfied that he'd saved as much of the map as he could, Bruce marched over to where Alex was now picking up more clothing. At that moment, another gust blew his daughter's bra into his face. And now I'm the number one clip on YouTube, he thought, as he saw several of his amused staff pointing their camera-phones at him. He wondered whether *Egypt's Funniest Home Videos* offered a cash prize. God knows, the dig needed all the funding it could get.

Gingerly, Alex took the underwear in one hand. "Thanks," she said. "It's clean... if that helps."

"Not particularly, Alex. When I said I wished we were closer, this is not what I had in mind."

Meekly, she passed him a washcloth.

"Forget it," he said. "They're clean, right? Actually, you know what? I think I *will* take it. It's about two o'clock, right?"

"What's that got to do with it?"

"See that cloud?"

Alex turned her head to see that there was indeed a large dust cloud heading for them.

"Wow. Is that natural, Dad?"

"Not in the slightest," he replied, resignedly.

As it grew closer, the sound of an automobile engine became apparent. Bruce thrust his wristwatch in front of her face.

"See that? Two o'clock, right on schedule." He gave a deep sigh, and helped Alex to her feet.

The cause of the cloud, a black Rolls Royce, flew through the sand and stopped right in front of them.

A face full of dust sent Alex into a coughing fit. Her father appeared unmoved. He simply wiped himself with the cloth and handed it back to her.

"Thanks. I see what you mean now."

"Don't mention his nose."

"Whose nose?"

"You'll see."

Looking to Alex like something from the kind of Agatha Christie TV movie she usually lost patience with before the solution, a driver in full livery got out, and opened the passenger door to reveal a huge shaven-headed Egyptian who, despite his elegant clothing, looked like he'd be more at home in a WWF arena than a vintage Rolls. His bent nose suggested a violent brawl somewhere in his past.

"What the hell is going on here, Stone?" he barked. "What is this child doing at my dig?"

Bruce's shoulders tensed involuntarily at his use of the phrase "*my* dig."

"She's my daughter, Mr Ahmed," he replied, watching his hefty backer struggle from the vehicle. "Alex, please meet Mr Ahmed."

Alex put her hand out, but Ahmed simply walked right past her, giving no indication that he had even seen it. Considering the number of people who had offered her their hand recently – mostly to pick her up whenever she fell on her ass – it seemed extremely rude.

Despite the obvious slight to his own flesh and blood, Bruce rushed after Ahmed.

"So what have you found so far, Doctor?"

"It's all very favourable," Bruce replied, hoping he sounded convincing, all the while rubbing his arm nervously. "We discovered that the map coordinates are off."

"They're what?"

"Off. Incorrect. That means-"

"It means I'm losing money, and it should be apparent to you by now that losing money is against my religion. So, Doctor..." He spun around on his heel to face Bruce, "do I need to hire someone else to do your job?"

"No, sir. You do not," Bruce told him, disguising his anger poorly. It had been bad enough that Ahmed claimed the dig as his own, but now being forced to address him as "sir" was the final kick in the nuts. At least, that's what he told himself. But he secretly knew that the kicks would keep on coming.

"I'll be back tomorrow, and you better have something for me, Stone." Ahmed may have sneered at the point, but his expression was never pleasant to look at, so it was hard to say for certain.

Before returning to his car, Ahmed tipped his hat to Rachel – an apparently gentlemanly gesture, but it merely added emphasis to his earlier diss. She gave him an obviously fake smile in return.

"Is he sensitive about his nose?" asked Alex, watching the Rolls speed away.

"Beats me," said Bruce. "But I figure it's so damn ugly, how could he not be?"

CHAPTER SIX

The evening meal was not conducted in silence, but silence would probably have been preferable to the long, painful gaps between mundane observations.

"How's the soup?"

Pause.

"Fine. How's yours?"

Pause.

"Fine. It's the same as yours."

Pause.

"Oh." Pause. "Right."

And so on. No-one visiting the campsite at that moment could have mistaken Alex or Bruce for Noel Coward.

Fusani watched from a distance, apparently unaware of any tension between the two members of the Stone family, even though Alex's expression soured as Rachel walked by, and waved.

"See you guys in the morning," she said.

Bruce waved back; Alex – despite receiving similar treatment from Ahmed - ignored her. Rachel seemed not to notice.

"So, she just follows you around like that all day, huh?" asked Alex, dully.

"As my assistant, yes, that would be part of her job." A final spoonful of soup passed his lips.

"I bet that makes the day go by fast."

Pause.

Bruce set down his empty bowl. "Alex, Rachel is my colleague on this trip."

"God, Dad, you are so blind!" Alex slammed her own bowl into the ground, spilling the contents. She had hardly touched it. "You have no clue what's going on, ever!"

Bruce adjusted his glasses, in the hope that it would give him the appearance of some authority. "Alex, of course I know what's going on around me."

"No, you just think you do. Dad, you live in this fantasy world where you try to make things the way *you* want them to be!"

"Oh, this is ridiculous!"

A loud slurping of soup alerted them both to the fact that Fusani was present, if seemingly oblivious to the family dispute going on before him.

"Grandma told me you still sleep with mom's pillow," Alex hissed.

"I'm sorry; did I miss the moment this conversation turned into a psychiatric evaluation? I thought *I* was the only *Dr* Stone at this excavation."

"You need to open your eyes, Bruce, and stop pretending."

Bruce's eyes bulged. He'd taken enough from Ahmed already today, but to be called "Bruce" by his own daughter...

"Since when did that start?" he asked, flustered. "No, no, you don't call me...*no*."

"You only came up to the school twice this year."

"In case you haven't noticed, Alex, I've been pretty busy."

"Yeah? Meanwhile, I'm starting to feel like I've lost both parents."

Too much. Bruce could do nothing but stare at her, like a man in shock. What was there to say? A retort? He just looked at the ground, as he always did when searching for answers. And, typically, he could see nothing there.

"Dad, I'm sorry..."

He looked up, seeing the regret on her face.

"No, I am," he snapped. He got to his feet suddenly. Alex rose, too, and seemed for a moment as though she might attempt to hug him. But all she managed in the end was to pat his elbow listlessly. It wasn't much, Bruce felt, but it was something.

"Alright," he announced, "you, uh, you should get some rest. You've had a long day. You know which tent is yours, right?"

"Mm-hm."

"Great. And don't stay up too late, reading your teen-bop magazines or whatever..."

This comment generated the first smile he'd seen since he and Alex had been reunited (and before she'd set eyes on Rachel).

"I don't think anyone says 'teen-bop' any more, Dad. In fact, I'm not sure anyone ever has."

Bruce frowned. "I used to say it. Am I that out of touch?"

Another smile. Maybe things were finally looking up.

***

Alex slept astonishingly well that night. She was amazed at herself the next morning, when she realised that when she'd closed her eyes, the possibility of creatures bigger than spiders finding their way into her tent had never even occurred to her. There were snakes in Egypt, right? Of course there were – one of them famously took out Cleopatra. Yes, her dad assured her that was historically inaccurate, but she was pretty sure that didn't mean there weren't any snakes. From now on, she'd have to know what might be slithering around in all possible directions.

As a result, it took her quite a while to reach her dad at the site of the giant hole, where he was busy counting out items of equipment. Fusani, leaning against the table while reading a hieroglyphic chart, paid her no heed. Bruce, however, glancing up to see his only child rotating very slowly on the spot, found it hard not to be reminded of a chicken on a spit.

"You'll never turn into Wonder Woman unless you pick up the pace a little," he noted.

"I don't get it." She stopped moving.

"The TV show with JoAnna Cameron. No, wait, it was Lynda Carter."

"I never heard of either of them."

"God, I'm old. Look, Alex, you should avoid getting dizzy, unless you want to fall down that hole. What are you doing, anyway?"

"Something just told me to... watch out for snakes. Pretty dumb, huh?"

"Sometime, I'll tell you my ten best snake anecdotes."

"Herpetology 101. Sounds like fun." For the first time, she noticed the flashlights and brushes laid out before her dad.

"What, no whip? You know, Shannon calls you Indiana Jones."

"Oh, yeah? Awesome. Shannon's your friend, right? The one you told me about?"

A thought occurred to her. "You weren't going to start without me, were you, Dad?"

He shrugged. "I remember your personality in the mornings, and I thought it best that you sleep in. You should feel privileged. They don't get the same consideration."

Alex was on the brink asking who "they" might be before she realised that many other members of the archaeological crew had gathered around her. In the heat, it was tough to tell that she reddened with embarrassment. Had they all been watching her acting like a dork, albeit it a justifiably cautious dork? To make matters worse, these were the same people who'd watched her running around the desert desperately trying to retrieve her undies. There was a big danger of them getting the wrong impression of her. Unfortunately, there was an even bigger danger of them getting the *right* impression. If anyone mentioned it, she'd say it was just a phase she was going through. Unfortunately, she knew, the phase was known as existence.

Perhaps the crew were aware that their jobs depended on not pissing off the boss, and upsetting his daughter would be an excellent way of achieving this. So nobody said anything, which, after her experiences at Northwood Boarding School, where her fellow pupils were never shy about voicing their opinion of her, actually seemed slightly worse.

"Alright," Bruce announced, "you all know which teams you've been assigned to. I want Team One to get down there and start tunnelling through."

A few crew members instantly grabbed their equipment and begin lowering themselves into the hole.

"Team Two, back them up and make sure the sand *clears* the hole."

Alex heard a few chuckles, and guessed that this must be what passed for humour in the archaeological world.

She watched Bruce leaned over Fusani's shoulder and nod, impressed at whatever the boy was doing. Fusani flashed another winning smile, and for a second, her glance caught his. Thank God she was already blushing. She should look busy, professional. Pretending to be unaware that Fusani was still watching her, she began searching through the gear like a pro, finally picking out a flashlight and brush that seemed more to her liking than the others. She decided to risk a glance at Fusani, but found her view of him blocked by Rachel. Alex hadn't even seen her arrive, but now that she was here, she didn't look too happy. She could guess why. Come to that, she wasn't too happy to see Rachel either.

"We should get going, Bruce," the woman said, placing her hand on his shoulder. Alex pretty much hated that she called her father by his first name.

"So," Alex asked him, pointedly ignoring Rachel, "which team am I on?"

Bruce exhaled audibly. "Actually, Alex, while we're down in the tunnel, I was wondering if you could perform another task."

"Uh, OK. What is it?"

"We're in desperate need of firewood."

Nobody spoke for a while.

"Firewood?"

"Firewood. It's very important, Alex."

She felt anger well up inside her, and although she knew Rachel to be the cause, her annoyance was nevertheless directed at her father.

"Whatever," she said airily. "You guys go off and have a huge adventure, and I'll just go collect wood."

"Alex..."

"Who do you think I am, Dad, Arthur Dent?"

"Is that someone from your school?"

"It's a character from a book," Rachel offered, before Alex got a chance.

"Yeah, he was stuck on the surface of an alien planet while his friends got to explore beneath the surface."

"I really don't see the see what you're getting at, Alex," he said.

"Yeah, that seems to be happening a lot, *Bruce*." He didn't react to that, so Alex began to mutter under her breath, almost daring her father to demand, "What was that, young lady?"

But he didn't. Instead, he simply threw his pack over his shoulder, before instructing Fusani: "Finish up those glyphs, then check on... you know." It was painfully obvious to Alex that she was the "you know" that needed checking on. And while she had drifted off to sleep the night before entertaining thoughts of being checked on by the young Egyptian, now his attentions would only increase her fury.

She didn't even wait to see Bruce and Rachel shimmy down the hole. Instead, she marched off in search of wood. If they wanted wood, she'd find them wood, a whole damn forest, if she could. Teams One and Two would climb out of the hole, and they'd be like, "Hey, I can't see! There's all this wood in our way! Where did it all come from?" And Alex would just be sitting there, a cool drink her hand, and she'd simply say, "Oh, I did that. You said you wanted firewood, right? Is that enough, because I could get more." God, she was so awesome in her fantasy life. In the real world, it turned out, gathering scraps of wood was a titanic pain in the ass. After an hour, she had gathered about a dozen pieces - a long way off the "whole damn forest" she'd pictured. But it was something. It showed she wasn't completely worthless. Not completely.

That notion gave Alex no reassurance as, turning round to head back to camp, she instantly tripped over a branch embedded in the sand, causing her to fall flat on her face, scattering her collected pieces of wood in all directions. She thumped the ground in frustration, something she'd always thought people only did in movies.

"Shit!"

Alex didn't want to cry, but she couldn't stop the tears from coming. She just couldn't seem to get anything right, and when she tried to do something useful, she got tripped up by a stupid branch. And to make matters worse, she was somehow trapped by it. She tried twisting her foot left and right, but couldn't get it loose.

"Oh, come on!" she cried. She supposed she could scream for help, but there was no guarantee Fusani would even hear her, and besides, she wasn't prepared to submit herself to further humiliation if she could avoid it. No, if she could just get her hands around it, imagine it was Rachel's neck and throttle it... It occurred to her at the last moment that it was actually a root rather than a branch, but the sand around her had already begun to move. The knowledge that she had discovered a sinkhole was her last coherent thought for some time.

Back at the site a few minutes later, Fusani decided that he'd better do as Dr Stone said and make sure the American girl hadn't gotten herself into any trouble.

CHAPTER SEVEN

Once her coughing and sneezing fit had subsided, and she was confident she'd spit up as much of the sand in her lungs as she was able, Alex took a few minutes to check herself over. She was pretty certain there wasn't a part of her body that hadn't been injured in the fall. If there was anything internal that had survived unscathed, it was probably something she could live without, like her appendix. Maybe the fact that her crappy mood had returned was a good sign; she couldn't have sustained any serious head injuries if she had the sense to realise how thoroughly screwed she was right now.

No, the only thing that wasn't working satisfactorily was her left ankle. She had landed hard on it, when she had arrived wherever the hell she was – not Wonderland, she figured. Alice, so far as she could remember, had enjoyed a relatively stress-free descent, and landed without even a smudge on her pinafore. Alex, of course, wasn't wearing a pinafore, but her clothes were both filthy and blood-stained, from the many scratches her hands and face had sustained as she had fallen.

Back in Mr Willowby's history class, Alex had longed for a hole to swallow her up. Having experienced it, she couldn't in all honesty recommend it. By now, the dust thrown up by her collision with the ground had settled, and she could see where she had landed.

"Holy crap," she whispered. "I'm in a tomb."

Beautiful hieroglyphics covered the walls, and she could just about make out an ornate gold and black sarcophagus leaning against the far wall.

I did it, she thought. Two teams of trained archaeologists, including my dad and the hated Rachel are tunnelling under the Great Pyramid, and I, Alex Stone, girl genius and future President of the United States, discovered it single-handedly...

With growing horror, she realised that a hand was, at present, resting on her shoulder. A cold, bony hand. Too terrified to move, she slowly turned her head to discover that reason the hand seemed bony was because it was composed entirely of bones and nothing else. A skeleton was hanging out of a gold and blue sarcophagus behind her, as though either trying to make its escape or pull her inside with it. Either prospect terrified Alex, and, quite understandably, she screamed till her lungs ached and she began coughing violently once again. After a few minutes of this, it became clear that the skeleton, whoever it might once have been, meant her no harm. Not much comfort, she considered, since I'm stuck in a tomb with a skeleton for company. If she'd paid more attention when *CSI* was on, she'd know whether she was in the company of a male or female corpse. On closer inspection, she decided female. The golden breastplate seemed to have been designed to accommodate... well, breasts. Of the female variety. And the jewel-encrusted bracelet hanging from the wrist? Definitely a woman. The ancient Egyptians definitely had a thing for bling.

"Who *were* you?" Alex whispered.

Weird, but she was transfixed by that bracelet. There was something about it... Those jewels, were they glowing? The tomb certainly appeared brighter than before. She reached out to the skeleton, mesmerized. Unable to control her actions, Alex found herself pulling the bracelet from the dead woman's wrist. It came off surprisingly easily. Perhaps a little large for her own arm, she noted absently as she put it on. As though reading her thoughts, the bracelet seemed to shrink down and lock into place. Alex was suddenly in charge of herself again, and finding herself in great pain, she began to panic. She scratched furiously at the object, but it refused to move, as though it were somehow welded to her skin. No use. A high, whining sound assaulted her ears. It grew louder the more she struggled. Now it was in her head, tearing her brain apart. Dizziness overtook her. She stumbled backwards, colliding with the other sarcophagus. The last thing she saw before passing out, was that she had accidentally knocked open its lid, and a steady stream of dust was now spilling onto the floor of the tomb.

***

"Maybe she needs mouth-to-mouth," a familiar Egyptian voice suggested.

"She's breathing just fine, Fusani. Get me a damp towel. God, this is my fault. Come on, sweetheart, come back to me."

Opening her eyes proved to be more of a challenge than Alex expected, until she realised they were probably glued shut with dried blood from the cut on her head. I wonder if this is a good look for me, she thought. When she was at last able to see again, she was surprised to discover that she was no longer in the tomb, but back above ground again. I suppose the heat of the sun on my skin should've been a tip-off.

"Hi, Dad," was all she could think of to say.

"Thank God!" he gasped, hugging her tightly.

"Found me, huh?"

"I heard you screaming," Funsani volunteered, and handed her the towel.

"I must've been pretty loud. What exactly happened to me?"

"Never mind, Alex," her father replied, "you're fine now. I'm going to call Oceanic and book a flight back home for you. What the hell was I thinking?"

Upon hearing this, Alex was suddenly completely alert. "No, Dad, I want to stay here!"

"Alex, Egypt is a very... intense place, and I don't think you can handle it. I mean, look at yourself."

As instructed, Alex glanced over her cuts and bruises, and to her swollen ankle. True, it didn't look good. But she wasn't going to let that stop her.

"No, I'm staying here. This is so typical of you! Every time something gets too difficult, you just dismiss it."

"I'm not dismissing you."

At the sound of running, Alex attempted to raise herself up onto her elbows, but Fusani prevented it. "No," he said. "Stay where you are. Don't excite yourself."

This last piece of advice was worth taking, given that one of the pairs of feet she'd heard turned out to belong to Rachel, and Alex already felt herself beginning to seethe.

"Oh my God, Alex, what happened?" Rachel gasped, somehow suggesting irritation and concern in about equal measure.

"She found the tomb," Fusani replied, flatly. And that shut everyone up for a second.

"Alex, is that true?" Bruce asked.

Trying to sound as casual as possible in the situation, Alex said, "Well, there were some paintings on the walls and two sarcophaguses. Is that the plural?"

"Sarcophagi," corrected Fusani.

"'Kay, Sarcophagi. Thanks, Fusani. There you have it. Tomb."

Her father was flabbergasted. "But that's impossible. According to the Stela, it should be over there..." He pointed, which, to Alex, laid flat on the ground, was no help at all.

"Well, it's not," she stated. "Um... Surprise? I guess."

With a sudden intensity with which Alex would never have credited him, Bruce practically grabbed Fusani and demanded to be shown the discovery. Sooner or later, she'd have to fess up to the fact that she hadn't so much discovered the tomb as fallen into it with all the grace she displayed in any of her athletic endeavours at Northwood. But right now, she was enjoying her moment in the limelight.

Or, at least, she had been enjoying it up until the moment she realised that she had been abandoned by everyone. Wow, I am literally less popular than a hole, she thought. If I'd had any ego left, that would've just about destroyed it. Nobody seemed to care anymore whether she got up or not, so what was stopping her anymore?

When she saw Rachel shimmy down the rope, on her way to verify the discovery, she wished she hadn't bothered. Limping over to the hole, she heard a loud whoop of joy from within. That whoop? *I* did that, she told herself. Of course, I also robbed a tomb, but- But what? Why hadn't she mentioned the bracelet? Why had she even tried it on in the first place? An ancient Egyptian bracelet in an underground crypt? That can't be sanitary. At least it didn't hurt any more. In fact, it felt just fine.

It was as she fingered the bracelet cautiously, that her father unexpectedly turned away from the hole and noticed her new accessory for the first time.

"Where did you get that?" he asked.

Automatically, she pulled down her sleeve to cover it up. "I got it from a street vendor at the market."

"Bazaar."

"Yeah, pretty wild," she agreed.

"No, not 'bizarre', 'bazaar'."

"Right. That thing you just said. That's where I got it. In Giza." She tried very hard not to notice that Fusani was staring at her. He, of course, knew that she was lying; they hadn't stopped at any market, and she hadn't been wearing the bracelet before he had rescued her. No point in trying to figure out what he was thinking; she wasn't even sure what she herself was thinking.

"Let me have a look at that arm," Bruce demanded, suddenly grabbing her. Alex pulled back, more concerned that he would take a closer look at the bracelet.

"Ow, Dad, stop!" she cried, feigning pain. Now why did I just do that, she wondered? What's the worst that could happen? Apart from him being unbelievably pissed at me for disturbing the archaeological find of a lifetime? OK, that would be pretty bad, I guess.

Exasperated, he simply sighed. "Alright then, let's see just how good these Egyptian doctors are. Fusani, I want you to drive the jeep over here."

Fusani looked very much as though he had something to say.

"What?" Bruce asked. "What's on your mind?"

Oh Goddess, Alex thought, he's going to say something. Wait a second – *Goddess*? Where did *that* come from?

Before Fusani had the chance to speak, Rachel's head emerged from the hole behind them.

"Bruce, you've got to get down here!" For the first time since she had encountered this- this- Alex wasn't exactly sure what to call her. Not a home-wrecker, since her dad was hardly at home anyway. The point was, Rachel had finally performed a useful task by causing a significant distraction. She saw Bruce look longingly at the hole.

"Just go, Dad," she said.

He shook his head, as though coming out of a trance (something Alex could totally identify with). "What? No. We've got to get you to the hospital." His protests weren't particularly heart-felt, and for once this gave her a sense of relief rather than one of resentment.

"I can take her," Fusani suggested.

"Yeah, Fusani can take me. It's not like you'd understand what the doctors were saying anyways."

"Honey, are you sure you're OK with this?"

When he put it like that, she realised that she was less OK with it than she'd at first imagined. Who wouldn't want their dad with them when they visited an unfamiliar hospital in a foreign country? Or, come to that, any hospital in any country? But she'd put herself in this position, and it would certainly prevent any awkward questions about the bracelet, even though she knew she'd have to face them somewhere down the line.

"Yeah, go," she mumbled, unenthusiastically, "it's cool."

He gave her a monstrously firm hug before grabbing his tool belt, and dialling a number on his cell phone. "Dr Williams," he said, hardly giving the person on the end time to say hello, "you are about to become a very happy woman..."

Grimacing slightly, Alex turned to Fusani.

"Oh, Fusani," her rapidly departing father yelled, "make sure they x-ray her arm!"

"OK, Doctor." The young Egyptian helped Alex to the jeep, supporting her weight all the time.

"My dad thinks I'm helpless," she told him, not even caring whether he was paying attention. "And maybe I am. I can't even get firewood without causing a crisis."

"You know, Cleopatra was only seventeen when she ascended the throne," he remarked.

"Oh, yeah? And I thought I had a lot to deal with."

"I'm sure she made many mistakes, but she is not remembered for them."

"No, she's remembered for being bitten by a snake. Although that probably didn't happen, y'know."

He smiled, and she suddenly felt a whole lot better. Or, at least, she did until she noticed a cloud of dust heading their way.

"Is it two o'clock already?" She asked. "Wow, I *was* out for a long time."

It was about a minute before the familiar Rolls Royce became visible.

"The generous Mr Ahmed," Fusani observed. "We're leaving just in time."

CHAPTER EIGHT

For the Colombia University archaeological team, the discovery was like Christmas. The fact that they were celebrating this particular Christmas in an ancient tomb troubled none of them, which probably tells you all you need to know about archaeologists.

Bruce and Rachel were engrossed in overseeing the transit of a large stone tablet covered in both hieroglyphics and jewels of, no doubt, fabulous value. As two crew members hoisted the tablet out of the tunnel, a large corner broke off with a snap like a gunshot. Bruce managed to catch the segment before it hit the ground and smashed into even smaller pieces.

"Excuse me," he said with a brittle tone, "but could we exercise a little more caution, people? I shouldn't have to tell you that these artefacts are extremely fragile."

Both crew members apologised, embarrassed.

"Just deliver it to the lab in one piece, please. I mean, deliver that piece in one piece. I'll keep this piece."

He intended to shoot Rachel a wearied glance, but was surprised to find that she was no longer close by. Looking around the tomb, he saw her studying the gold and blue sarcophagus.

"This is unbelievable!" he announced, approaching her. "We finally have tangible proof that my hypothesis has merit."

It seemed to Bruce that she was now seemed more interested in the skeleton than anything he had to say. Given her usual enthusiasm, he was surprised to realise that he found her diffidence rather troubling.

"Who do you suppose she was?" she asked.

"'She'?" He examined the battle armour, intact after thousands of years. "Yes, I suppose so."

"Bruce, you don't really suppose it's... Isis, do you?"

He knew what he wanted to believe, but common sense took hold at last. "No, it couldn't possibly be. What about the other one?" He nodded toward the gold and black sarcophagus.

"Nothing but dust."

"Right. I think that's enough for right now. Come on, everybody, we're calling it a day."

He could tell that Rachel was uneasy about leaving, and he understood her reluctance. But it had been a hell of a day, and he was just as concerned about his daughter as he was about the find. No, more concerned. Probably. No, definitely. Definitely more concerned.

"I can promise you, Rachel, this tomb will still be here tomorrow. It's waited thousands of years for us to find it, what's one more day?"

Rachel smiled, which cheered him immensely.

***

The first sight that greeted Bruce upon reaching the surface was that of Ahmed, seated in a deck-chair, a napkin resting on his lap as he helped himself to cakes and other small delicacies from a fragile-looking table at his side.

"Welcome back, Dr Stone." He smiled, revealing years of dental negligence. "I've been here for some hours, watching your people bring up artefacts, and load them onto trucks."

"I'm grateful for your vigilance," Bruce responded, without enthusiasm or an iota of truth.

"I must congratulate you. You are about to make a rich man even richer." He laughed, and his driver joined in. Bruce assumed that finding his Ahmed's jokes funny was a requirement of the job, which made their own working relationship seem less onerous by comparison.

"Glad I could be of service, but it was really a group effort. You should be thanking everyone."

"I don't believe I thanked anyone."

Bruce noticed that Ahmed wasn't meeting his gaze. He couldn't possibly be shy. Then he realised that the bloated Egyptian's attention was focused on the piece of tablet Bruce was still holding. No doubt he was entranced by the inlaid jewels. Yes, that would be typical of Ahmed.

"And what is that you hold?" Ahmed asked.

Idly, Bruce glanced down at the item in his hand, hoping he could convince Ahmed it was of no monetary value. Some hope. "It broke off a stone tablet, but possesses markings of the fourth Dynasty... as I predicted, incidentally."

Ahmed shot him a glare, then snapped his fingers. "Give. Give it to me."

Hiding his reluctance as best he could, Bruce handed it over. Ahmed grabbed at it eagerly, knocking a small pastry into the sand.

"I am going to have my own archaeologists analyse this, just to be sure."

This was going too far. "Mr Ahmed, you cannot," Bruce protested. "The stone tablet cannot be properly deciphered without that piece."

Once again, Ahmed glared at him. "Pardon me, but I am funding this dig, am I not? I tell you what to do, not the other way around."

Bruce was about to protest further, but Ahmed cut him off before he could make a sound. "Please, go on, Doctor... if you want to be released from this excavation."

Bruce could go on telling himself that Indiana Jones wouldn't put up with this crap, but he also knew that your average fictional archaeologist never had to worry about matters like funding. Anyone who routinely used a whip rarely had to worry about work relations issues. In the real world, as much as he hated admitting it, there were times when you just had to suck it up.

"No," he said. "I'm through."

"I thought so," Ahmed replied, with a hideous smile. God, Bruce thought, his teeth are more crooked than his nose.

***

So far as anyone at the camp was aware, the admittedly anticlimactic confrontation between Ahmed and Dr Stone was the last dramatic moment that long day presented. They could not have been more incorrect. Just before dawn, a figure emerged from the tomb. Had anyone been awake to see it, they would have judged it roughly human, though the massive dark cloak made it difficult to be certain. And surely no human ever had eyes that glowed so green. Nor would they have been so comfortable surrounded by scorpions.

Even if anyone had witnessed this extraordinary occurrence, they would never have had the courage to admit that they had seen Set, brother of Isis and Dark God of Chaos, rise again from the Tomb of the Gods....

CHAPTER NINE

As Alex awoke, she wondered why there were crutches in her bedroom. Had she been hurt at school? And when did she decide to turn the bed around? And buy a plant? A few seconds later, full clarity returned and she remembered that she was not in her room at Northwood; she was not even in America any longer. In fact, she wasn't a hundred per cent certain of the name of the person this place belonged to. Some relative of Fusani's, she thought. Not a parent, she was pretty sure. At the time, her body had been a battlefield, with injuries and painkillers fighting it out. Fusani might as well have said, "This is the crack district, I might or might not be back for you," and she wouldn't have cared.

This was becoming a bad habit, she thought, waking up and wondering where she was. Maybe things would improve once she was back home. Who was she kidding? How could things possibly be better?

The noise of traffic outside her window was insanely loud. Had it been that way all night? How had she slept through it? Soundly, she guessed.

She leaned across for the crutches, and was aware for the first time of the bandages on her arms, another souvenir of her evening in the hospital. Had they had some kind of lotion on the bandages in Egypt? She felt just fine. Really fine. Epic, in fact. Whatever they'd put in that injection, it must still be working.

Well, no point staying in bed all day. Actually, that wasn't true, there was really no good reason to get up – hadn't she just fallen several feet and a few thousand years, necessitating stitches, bandages and crutches? Then again, right about now, Rachel was walking all over *her* tomb, and how many times had she credited Alex with the discovery? Zero, maybe? You better believe it.

Throwing off her bedclothes, Alex placed her feet gingerly on the floor, awaiting a sudden shooting pain in her ankle. But the pain never came. That wasn't the injections; it just didn't hurt any more. It was fine. Weird. She wouldn't actually need the crutches after all. A thought struck her. It was crazy, but... Her leg didn't hurt, right? And her arms felt OK, despite what the presence of bandages suggested. With a rapidity that surprised her, given her usual squeamishness, Alex tore the bandages off, to reveal... no scratches, no wounds, nothing. Just a pair of lean, muscular arms. Wait a second, when had her arms ever been muscular? And had someone done her nails while she slept? They'd never looked so glossy or unbitten. What the hell was happening to her? She reached for her forehead, remembering that blood had glued her eyes shut the day before. It must have been a big wound, but she now couldn't feel it. A mirror. She needed a mirror.

Her first reaction upon seeing the figure reflected in the full-length mirror was to emit a shriek. Not because her accident had turned her into a hideous deformity, but because she imagined someone must have sneaked into the room and was standing behind her. But if that was indeed the case, then why she couldn't see herself in the mirror, too? That was dumb. No, incredible as it seemed, the reflection was really her.

"Holy shit," was all she could think to say, which was a real pity, because the situation called for something more inspired. She was beautiful! She still looked like herself, but... beautiful. Her hair was now long and luxurious- no more frizz. She ran her fingers through it, feeling like she ought to be in a shampoo commercial. How could this be? Sure, she'd sometimes thought about getting a complete makeover – often after her usual style resulted in a football to the back of the head – but she didn't think it would be possible to sleep through one as intensive as this. Lifting up her pyjama top, she knew there was no way her waist could have reduced this much overnight, nor could she have just grown these rock-hard abs. No, something this awesome required a lot of hours in the gym and the kind of special equipment she'd only seen in infotainment ads hosted by ex-soap stars. There was only one other person she could think of who'd had this kind of experience, but Tobey Maguire's abs were CGI, weren't they?

She looked down. Oh my God, she thought, I totally have boobs! Real ones, not CGI! They were pretty big – not Kardashian big, but, you know, impressive. Would she be a pervert if she touched them, just for a second? Wow. What was in those things, cement? She wouldn't be surprised to find that they could deflect bullets, not that she'd ever want to put it to the test. It was pretty clear that the bra that'd hit her dad full in the face a couple of days earlier wouldn't be any good to her now.

Alex had had dreams like this, and had usually woken from them only to punch her mattress in frustration, knowing that she was the same old Alex after all. But never, in any of those dreams, had she ever questioned the reality of what had happened to her. It always seemed completely natural. She knew, then, that this could not be a dream. It didn't feel at all natural. And that fact that her first thought was that it must be a dream, told her that it definitely wasn't. This was really happening.

As she started to dress, she observed that the jewels on the bracelet were still emitting a soft pink glow. Oh crap, she thought, the bracelet! I got so caught up in how much I've changed, I totally forgot about it. How am I going to explain it to Dad? Actually, you know what? I think I already have enough to explain for the time being. I can just leave the bracelet here for a day or two. Maybe three or four.

But for some reason she couldn't fathom, she just couldn't get it off. Was it welded to her skin or something? No, that was crazy. Right. As crazy as everything else that had happened to her in the past twenty-four hours.

She jumped at the sound of a knocking on the bedroom door. Looks like I've only changed on the outside, she realised. I'm still the scaredy-cat I always was.

"Alex, how are you feeling?" It was Fusani. How to respond?

"Uhhh.... yeah." Pretty smooth. Obviously, the transformation hadn't expanded her vocabulary.

Slowly, the door opened a crack and she saw the young man's eyes widen as her caught sight of her new look. The door suddenly flew open.

"Wow."

Fidgeting nervously, she simply asked, "What?" Like she couldn't have guessed.

"Nothing," he replied, trying to hide his surprise. "Just... looks like you're feeling better. Do you feel better?"

As a matter of fact, she did. She felt a whole lot better, amazing even, but she had no idea how to convey the way she felt.

"Fusani, do I look different to you at all?"

Now he was the one who seemed not to know how to answer.

"Or is it just me?"

He shook his head frantically. "No, you definitely look different."

"I thought so, too. But in a good way, right?"

"Pretty good. I'd say. Pretty good."

CHAPTER TEN

Why, Bruce wondered, couldn't he entrust the mundane business of checking the batteries in the flashlights to anyone else? Wasn't this what they called micro-managing? He knew the reason was, of course, that he just didn't dare risk anything else going wrong when so much was at stake.

He was under fire from all sides, with Williams back at Colombia counting down the seconds until the expedition could be abandoned, and Ahmed right here in Egypt, who- Well, he wasn't actually sure what Ahmed's motivation was, but he knew he didn't trust the guy. Yes, he was obviously driven by wealth and the desire to increase that wealth, but there had to be easier ways to do it than fund a dig organised by an archaeologist who had pretty much tarnished any reputation he might once have possessed. It was a crazy situation, to say the least – without Ahmed's generosity, there was no way they could have travelled to Egypt and made this extraordinary find. And yet, at the same time, Bruce considered Ahmed the man he liked and trusted least in the entire world. Archaeology makes strange bedfellows, he thought, then shuddered at the mental picture that sentence had inspired. Not even if I wanted to experiment, he decided, firmly.

"We should probably try to figure out that warrior's identity," a pleasingly feminine voice suggested.

"Mm-hm," Bruce responded. "And do you have any suggestions as to how we go about that, Rachel?"

"Maybe whoever occupied the other sarcophagus could give us a clue? I mean, I don't want to suggest that if she's Isis then the other one could have been her brother, Set-"

Bruce held up his palm to silence her. "I'm not even ready to think about that," he said. "Not with the academic community all ready to jump down my throat."

Rachel smiled. "Well, when you're proved correct, they can jump up your butt instead."

Bruce wanted to hug her right then and tell her that was exactly what he wanted to hear, but he was afraid of what might happen if he did. Try to focus on the task at hand.

"I, uh... I examined the hieroglyphics on the woman's armour, and what I don't understand is that the markings don't resemble those of the Second or Third Dynasty. They seem to be older than that."

"That would make her over four thousand years old, Bruce."

"Exactly."

"You know what Dr Williams will say."

Unfortunately, he knew precisely what she would say. She would question how human remains of such great age could be in the condition they were. That was something he was wondering about himself, especially when one considered that the occupant of the other sarcophagus was now nothing more than a heap of dust.

"I don't understand," he confessed. But then he realised that Rachel wasn't even listening to him. She wasn't looking at him, either. She was staring past him at something, like she was in shock. He turned, and saw someone who looked kind of like Alex, except-

"Oh-my-God."

With her hair blowing in the lazy Egyptian wind, she looked more like a model on a shoot than his daughter, but... But that was his daughter! And she looked amazing. Well, of course, she'd always been beautiful in his eyes, but- Oh, shut up, Bruce, he told himself. Still, she had to blossom sometime, but who knew puberty could happen overnight?

Fusani, who walked alongside her, seemed pretty happy with the results, too. If he's laid a finger on her, he thought...

"It seems like you had a good night's sleep, Alex," he observed, somehow restraining his fury.

"Yeah, I guess so," Alex beamed. "Maybe Egyptian hospital food agrees with me."

"And how are your injuries?" Rachel asked, though it was hard to tell whether she was genuinely concerned or merely perplexed.

"All gone," replied Alex. "It's amazing. See?"

She rolled up her sleeve to show them. Just like she'd said, there were no marks any more. No scratches, no bruises, nothing.

Bruce shook his head in bemusement. "I just can't quite comprehend-"

As though attempting to cut off any more questions, Alex simply said, "Well, I'm feeling much better, Dad. Do you think I could come on the dig with you today?"

"Well, I'm not sure..." he said, and he really wasn't. He was no longer sure about anything.

"Come on, I'll be safer in the tomb with you then out collecting firewood. Unless, you know, you're hoping I'll fall into another tomb. Is that really how archaeology is supposed to work?"

He found he just had to smile. She had a point, damn it. Nothing to do but capitulate. "Alright, alright," he said, holding up his hands in a gesture of defeat. "Just do me one favour, grab my clipboard from the tent."

"Sure."

As she ran off for the clipboard, Bruce watched Simon pass by, catch sight of Alex, and trip over the ropes of his tent, dropping the armload of shovels he'd been carrying.

Fusani seemed to find this extremely funny, but Bruce was not even slightly amused. "I don't think you've met my daughter, Simon," he said, coldly.

Simon gave a weak smile. "Oh. Sorry, Dr Stone, sir. Right, well, where do you want these shovels?"

"Next to the flashlights. That'll be fine."

"Aye, aye, Captain," he said, weakly, and began picking up shovels.

Now that Alex was out of sight, Bruce turned to Fusani. "Last night, at the hospital - exactly what kind of machine did they put her through?"

"X-ray," Fusani replied. "Why?"

"Honestly, I have no idea."

A sound like an explosion tore through the camp. Bruce, Fusani and Rachel all looked in different directions, attempting to identify the source of the extraordinary noise. Nearby camels stirred restlessly.

"What the hell just happened?" Bruce demanded.

***

What had just happened was this:

Entering her father's tent, Alex cringed at the sight of a pair of his boots, with the socks hanging out of them. A second later, she cringed once again as the smell reached her.

"Oh, that's nasty!" she complained. "I wonder how Rachel would feel if she knew about this." The thought struck Alex that Rachel might already know, but that was an idea she wasn't ready to deal with yet.

OK, her dad had said he needed a clipboard. A clipboard. She was surprised to learn that anyone apart from gym coaches still used them. Hadn't anyone here ever heard of the iPad? That gross Ahmed guy was supposed to be funding this operation, but it sure didn't look like he'd put his hands too deep into his pockets. Looking around on Bruce's desk, she noticed pictures of several ancient hieroglyphs. She hadn't noticed them in the tomb, so Alex guessed he must have brought them for research purposes. They seemed to show a man and a woman in battle – the woman looked fairly awesome, and kind of familiar in a way Alex couldn't quite put her finger on. Something about the breastplate, maybe?

Anyhow, this wasn't finding the clipboard. Probably, it was in her dad's satchel. Picking it up by the strap, she dropped it onto the desk, causing it to fall open and emit a cloud of dust. Alex stepped back, but she was too late to prevent it assaulting her nostrils, giving her no option other than to sneeze. Boy, was it a powerful sneeze. It sounded to her more like a gunshot, and it seemed to create a miniature whirlwind within the tent, which gathered up all of Bruce's papers. Anyone who had been looking in the right direction at that moment would have seen the tent swaying back and forth on its poles.

Did I just do that? Alex thought. And if I *did* do that, *how* did I do that? Picking up her dad's shaving mirror, she checked whether there might not be something up her nose. Nope, nothing. And anyway, what could possibly do something like this? No, she could be the only one who could have done it. But that didn't make any more sense. Had she acquired some insane super power? The ability to fire boogers that travelled faster than a speeding bullet? Impressive, but also impractical. And gross.

Before she could think too hard about any other bodily emissions capable of causing property damage, she noticed the clipboard poking out of the satchel and grabbed it.

Throwing back the flaps of the tent, she immediately bumped into Fusani. He eyed her suspiciously.

"Found it," she said, in an off-hand manner.

"Found it?"

"Clipboard. Found it."

He glanced down at the clipboard which presently obscured his view of her frankly amazing boobs.

"Did you hear that sound?" he mumbled.

"Sound? I heard... I mean, I don't- What did it sound like? This sound, I mean? Was it something like a gun going off, or a bolt of lightning? Like that?"

"No it was more like a really loud sneeze."

"A sneeze? No, I didn't hear anything like that. That would be really weird, wouldn't it?"

"Are you alright, Alex?"

"Yeah sure, I'm fine. I'm totally fine. Listen, I should've said it sooner, but- thank-you. For... you know. Stuff."

Feeling awkward beyond belief – that hadn't changed either, dammit - she hurried past him towards the excavation site. She could sense that Fusani was still staring at her. She wanted to thank him, most of all, for not telling her dad she had lied about where she'd acquired the bracelet. But she still wasn't sure why he had kept her secret. It couldn't be out of a desire to get to second base – there hadn't been a lot on offer then. So what was going on in his mind?

***

As Bruce delicately brushed the dust off of a set of hieroglyphics on the wall, Alex, hovering over his shoulder, covered her nose and mouth with her sleeves. The last thing she wanted was to take her only remaining parent's head off with a titanic sneeze. Or at the very least, deafen him for life.

In spite of her stated interest in her father's activities, she kept one beady eye on Rachel, and not for the usual reason that she didn't want her within five feet of her father; no, it was because Rachel was spending a lot of time focusing on the skeleton in the gold and blue sarcophagus. For some reason, that bugged her, too. God, now she was even declaring dead people off-limits for Rachel. Was there anyone she would feel comfortable with that skank talking to? Fusani, maybe? No, definitely not Fusani.

"Now Alex, you see what I'm doing here?"

It struck her that she hadn't been paying attention to what her dad had been saying or doing for some time now.

"Uh, yeah," she lied. "Do you think you could maybe show me again?"

"You mean with you listening to me this time? Why not?"

She looked down as he demonstrated his brushing action. "Very carefully. Then we use the Dust-off."

Alex grabbed the aerosol can at their feet. "Here you go."

"But only *after* we brush," he added.

"Right, right." Bruce took a step back, presenting Alex with the opportunity to try for herself. With her own brush, she began to work on the wall.

"Gently, Alex, Gently." He leaned in and slowed her hand.

"I've got it, Dad," she reassured him. Giving her a comforting kiss, he moved away and let her get on with it.

As Alex resumed brushing, she thought she heard a loud creak, like the door of a haunted house in a lame black and white horror movie, or an even lamer fairground ride. She turned around, to check where the sound was coming from, but no-one else in the tomb seemed to have noticed anything. Her dad was now with Rachel, supervising her sketch. Great, she thought. They can hear me sneeze, but they can't hear *that*. Although, if she was being completely honest, it was one hell of a sneeze. She picked up the aerosol can and was about to spray, when she heard the noise again.

"OK, there was no way you didn't hear-"

She shut up the instant she realised that what she had heard was the lid slowly sliding off the sarcophagus. It was about to fall... and hit Dad and Rachel!

Hardly a second seemed to pass between the moment Alex was about to run towards them, and the moment when she caught the lid, mere inches from their heads. Had she given it more thought, she probably wouldn't have been able to make up her mind which astonished her more – that incredible burst of speed, or the strength she apparently possessed.

Her father was dumbstruck. He watched open-mouthed as she leaned the lid against the wall without any apparent effort. Finally, the power of speech returned to him.

"Alex, how did you..?"

"I thought I heard something," she replied, as if that explained everything (or anything).

Putting it more coherently than her father, Rachel cried, "You saved our lives!"

Alex blushed. If she'd been a total bitch, she might have claimed that she was only trying to save her dad's life, and that Rachel's survival was an unhappy accident. But that wasn't true or fair. She didn't want to see Rachel get hurt, not really.

"How did you lift that sarcophagus lid?" Bruce asked. "It's pure gold."

"It is? I don't know. I just... caught it. It was like a reflex. It can't be that heavy, I mean gold's a pretty soft metal, right?" Alex wondered if they would they buy that. She didn't, but would they?

"Alex, it must weigh nearly five hundred pounds!" Rachel pointed out.

The words sank in. Five hundred pounds. Flustered, Alex ran her hand through hair. Still felt good. "Yeah, I, uh... I saw that on TV once," she began. "Yeah, yeah, yeah... this mother got, like, super strength when her little boy got stuck under a car. You read about stuff like that. I'm pretty sure."

Seemingly uncertain how to respond, Bruce gave his daughter one of his patented powerful hugs. To Alex, it didn't seem to hurt as much as usual.

"Alright then... well, these artefacts aren't going to unearth themselves. I guess we should get back to work."

Rachel, it seemed to Alex, wasn't entirely satisfied with the situation, but did as she was told, nevertheless.

CHAPTER ELEVEN

Alex had not been looking forward to her first night back at the campsite – she was not really the outdoors type, she'd always insisted – but she'd gone off to sleep in her tent pretty quickly again, probably because her subconscious knew that the longer she stayed awake, the more difficult questions she'd be expected to answer. She didn't know how much longer she'd be able to avoid giving answers – she didn't even know most of the answers herself – but if it could wait another day, then it definitely *would* wait.

As it turned out, it didn't wait as long as she had hoped. As the night entered its final phase, she was awakened by a scream.

***

It came from one of the members of the archaeological team, moments after his tent was visited by a tall figure cloaked in black robes, scorpions scurrying in the sand around him, as though they somehow obeyed his will.

When the figure left his tent moments later, wielding a blood-covered sabre, it was clear to all witnesses that the occupant of the tent would never scream again. Within seconds, other team members were coming out of their own tents to find out just what the hell was happening. They all stopped short, each one terrified by the menacing glow of Set's green eyes. As he raised his arm, moonlight glinted off his gold bracelet, and the scorpions at his feet suddenly went wild, as though under a spell. But no-one could have imagined the nature of that spell. And when those scorpions rapidly morphed into men, men with golden eyes and the giant stinging tail of a scorpion, those watching might have imagined, or wished, they *were* dreaming. There were a few agonising moments of silence, before the scorpion-men shrieked, streaming through the camp, lighting fires and attacking the onlookers, all of whom were too stunned to react until it was too late for them.

Fusani had not risen straight away, and had lain on the fringes of consciousness until the mass panic brought him back to wakefulness with a start. Shadows darted about on the other side of his tent, voices were raised in panic. He was about to get up and find out what the screaming was all about, when another crew member – a guy he knew only as Robbie – pushed in front of him.

"Stay here, son," he warned, creeping cautiously towards the tent flaps.

A second later, a giant scorpion tail ripped through the tent, stabbing him in the chest and emerging from his back, between the shoulder blades. Fusani jumped back, as Robbie screamed out in pain. His attacker, half-man half-scorpion, entered the tent, pausing to stare down at the convulsing victim. While the creature wasn't looking, Fusani backed up, and crawled under the tent.

Alex, meanwhile, was sat in her bed, the sheet up to her neck. Her eyes widened in terror when the flap of her tent opened. She wanted to scream...

"Alex! It's me!"

Where her father had got the shotgun from, she didn't want to imagine.

"Dad! What's going on?"

"Some rebel faction. Egypt isn't exactly politically stable. You dig up parts a tomb some people consider sacred, you don't make yourself too welcome. That's what this is for." He held up the gun, not that there was a chance in a million of her not having already spotted it.

"Are you crazy? We should just leave!"

"It's a little late for that. I'm so sorry I brought you into this, honey. I want you to stay exactly where you are. I'm going to protect you, I swear-"

Any tenderness in the moment was utterly destroyed by Alex's scream as one of Set's scorpion-men burst into the tent, golden eyes fixed intently on her. Bruce swung around to face the intruder. Alex screamed again and covered her eyes as a deafening explosion filled the small tent. When she plucked up the courage to look, she saw her dad lowering his shotgun, the intruder writhing face down on the ground before them.

Pinchers, Alex thought, shocked. He has pinchers, like a scorpion. Wait, do I mean pinchers or pincers? Who cares, he's some kind of a freak. And so am I.

Bruce attempted to turn the would-be attacked over, but the instant the butt of his weapon touched the body, it disintegrated before their eyes. Within seconds, the dust that had previously been the scorpion-man was now indistinguishable from the Egyptian sand beneath his feet. "What the hell..?" breathed Bruce. "Definitely not a rebel faction."

"Dad..?"

Bruce did not look up. "Yes, honey?"

"What kind of gun is that?"

Whatever type it was, he didn't waste a moment in reloading. At the sight of the tent flaps opening once more, he raised his gun, ready to fire. Rachel shrieked at the sight of Bruce aiming a weapon at her. He let out a groan of relief.

"Rachel! Thank God!"

"Bruce, what is going on?" she demanded, clearly terrified. "Why is this happening?"

This was no time for stupid resentments, Alex realised. She held out her arms, and Rachel fell into them, sobbing.

Shrieks and screams were still coming from the remaining crew members outside. Whatever was happening, it was a massacre. Why it was happening was another question, but Alex was horrifyingly certain it could only be because of the bracelet. When the scorpion-man had entered the tent, he barely noticed her father. He was there for her, she knew it.

At last, all was silence. A silence that could only mean that the invaders had succeeded, and everyone else was dead. I want to believe they'll just leave us alone, Alex thought. Oh God, I want to believe it. Pleasepleasepleasepleaseplease.

She realised that the adults must be thinking the same thing, since all three of them were staring fixedly at the tent flaps, expecting the worst...

But when the worst came, it came from above. A massive sabre slashed through the nylon, and Alex had to push Rachel away before her head was sliced in two like a breakfast cantaloupe. She saw a pair of fiercely glowing green eyes staring down at her. Not at the others, just her.

Alex's screams mingled with those of Rachel and her father, as a few more slices of the sabre reduced the tent to ribbons. Now, they were out in the open, with nothing but a tent pole to offer them any protection, facing Set and ten of his scorpion-men, all waiting to spring.

"I promise I'll never kill a bug again," Alex squeaked.

CHAPTER TWELVE

Bruce put his arms in front of Alex and Rachel, attempting to somehow protect them both. Set, however, was clearly only interested in one member of the group.

To Alex, he was every inch the movie villain, his cloak revealing only a little of his shaven head and thin face, with its soulless green eyes. His expression had badass written all over it, even if his sabre and army of mutant supermen hadn't already got that point across.

"And here we are again, sister," he rasped.

As a greeting, it sounded every bit as sinister as "Hello, Sidney, what's your favourite scary movie?", but it didn't make a bit of sense.

"What?" Alex said.

Set reached his hand out. "Now give me the bracelet, and I shall see that you die with mercy."

"What bracelet?" Bruce asked, confused.

Oh, this is so not the time, thought Alex.

Thankfully, her dad didn't pursue the matter. "Stand back!" he told her, and fired his shotgun directly into Set's chest. The bullet bounced off, and was lost somewhere in the desert.

The scorpion-men shriek in unison, the same shriek they had emitted prior to massacring the entire camp. All ten lurched forward, ready to pounce.

At what felt to Alex like the last second, Set held up his hand, and his troops stopped, falling silent.

"You're making me very angry, Isis," he said, with chilling calm.

"Isis?" she repeated. "No, no, you're making a huge mistake. I'm not Isis. My name is- it doesn't matter, it wouldn't mean anything to you. But I'm not Isis!"

Alex looked pleadingly at her dad, who fired at Set again. Again, unsurprisingly, the bullet bounced off.

This time it was Rachel's turn to step forwards. "Look... sir. We don't mean any harm. If there's something you want, I'm sure we can give it to you." She held out a hand to him, a gesture of goodwill. Alex was astonished to see Set mimic the gesture... until he grabbed her by the wrist and threw her face-first into the tent pole.

"God damn you!" Bruce yelled.

In those moments before the sun was about to rise, the last thing that should have captured the attention of all participants in the standoff at this point was the appearance of a seventeen year-old Egyptian boy, approaching them across the sands. But somehow, Fusani managed to come perilously close to the invaders, close enough to look Set in the eye.

"*We call forth the powers of Isis to protect us from evil and lead us to safety,*" he chanted, over and over again.

Alex saw that with each repetition of these words, the bracelet around her wrist glowed ever brighter – not pink this time, but a brilliant red.

Set noticed too, and smiled. It was not a pleasant smile at all. "Now I shall finally end what we began so long ago."

The first rays of the sun peeked over the horizon. "How beautiful the morning light is," Set continued, ominously. "Wouldn't you agree, sister?"

Alex shuddered with fear as the Dark God caressed her cheek. His fingers were cold, colder than the desert nights. It was like being molested by a corpse. Then, without warning, he pulled up his cloak and fled, at a speed so great that Alex and the others were blinded by the sand thrown up in his wake. As though affected by his sudden absence, the scorpion-men morphed back into their original form and scurried after their leader. No-one felt much like stopping them.

A day ago, I was scared of snakes, thought Alex. I never thought about scorpions. And I especially never thought about scorpions that turn into guys with golden eyes and giant tails.

Bruce breathed a sigh of relief. Then realization struck. "Oh my God, Rachel!"

"I'm fine, I think," said Rachel, as he helped her to her feet. "Maybe a little concussion. Does anybody know what just happened?"

Alex checked her bracelet. It continued to burn red. She was surprised it didn't singe her flesh. But in fact, it felt just fi-

"'Street vendor', huh?"

She looked up to see her dad scowling down at her.

"You have some explaining to do, Alex. Where did you really get that?"

She winced. This moment was bound to come, she'd always known that, and there was only one thing to do under these circumstances – lie through her teeth.

"No, I did get from a vendor, I swear! Ask Fusani!"

"Alex, we were almost killed because of that bracelet. We all of us have the right to know."

That was undeniable, but bringing Rachel into it only seemed to make her admission more agonising.

"Alright, alright. This is going to sound worse than it is, but... I kind of swiped it from that skeleton."

If she had confessed to shooting one puppy a day, every day for the whole of her life up to that point, the reaction couldn't have been greater.

"You took an artefact?" Bruce managed, at last, to say.

"Kind of."

"Alex, how could you?" Rachel asked in a hurt tone. On any other subject, Alex's response would certainly have been, "You're not my mom!" But she knew she was in too deep for that now.

"I didn't mean to, I was just- drawn to it."

"It's not like clothes shopping, Alex," her dad chided. "You can't just pick something out because it's shiny."

"It actually wasn't that shiny when I- forget I said that."

Bruce held out his hand. "That is an incredibly important artefact. I don't have to tell you how incredibly disappointed in you I am. I think it's time you give it back."

"Yeah, about that... The thing is... I can't."

"What do you mean you can't?" Rachel asked.

"It won't come off. It's like it's glued on." She gave a tug on it by way of demonstration. "See? Won't budge."

"Let me try." He yanked hard on the bracelet, and Alex could see her skin stretch beneath it (which hurt less than she would have imagined), but still it wouldn't come off.

"You need to get your nails under it," Rachel suggested, but her attempts weren't any more successful than Bruce's. Alex wondered whether Fusani was going to offer his assistance, but he seemed entirely unsurprised by their repeated failure.

"Well this is just fabulous, Alex," Bruce scowled. "Now what?"

"I guess I become part of the exhibit. At least if I were in a glass case the whole time, you'd know I wasn't getting into any trouble." Her weak smile was not returned. Instead, her dad turned to face Fusani.

"What was that you yelled out before? When Dr Doom was about to kill all of us?"

"An incantation evoking the goddess Isis," Fusani replied, flatly.

"Are you telling us that Isis got rid of those... creatures?" Rachel asked him.

Fusani simply nodded.

"That's ridiculous!" Bruce almost spat out the words.

"Your daughter Alex wears the Bracelet of Isis."

"I do what now?" Alex asked.

"According to legend," her father began, "whoever possesses the bracelet inherits the strength, beauty, and agility of the warrior goddess."

Alex took in this information, considered it for a moment. "Come on, you don't really believe that crap, do you?" she said eventually.

Fusani and Rachel said nothing. Bruce's jaw agitated as though words were attempting to fight their way out, but nothing made all the way to his mouth.

"Dad, I don't know what those things were, but there's no way this 'Bracelet of Isis' stopped them."

"How else do you explain why you're totally hot now?" Fusani enquired. Bruce glared at him. "It's true, Dr Stone. I heard the phrase on *90210*; I'm using it right, aren't I?"

Alex no longer knew what to say. Her parents were scientists, and while she hadn't inherited their sense of adventure, she at least possessed a strong respect for the strictly factual, and a disdain for the completely impossible. But this morning, she had witnessed at least six impossible things, and she hadn't even had breakfast yet.

"Alex, can I see your bracelet?" Rachel requested.

"I thought you already saw it. You know, when you were trying to tear my arm off a second ago."

Rachel's voice was soft, almost reassuring. "I just want to examine it. I'll be gentle. Please."

With a petulant exhalation she knew was beneath her, Alex held out her wrist, allowing Rachel to inspect it.

Bruce, meanwhile, surveyed what had once been their campsite. After a few moments spent attempting to see any signs of life other than the four of them, he announced, "Pack your suitcases, we're going home. Fusani, unless there's somewhere you can stay where you know you'll be safe, you're coming with us, kid." He set off through the devastation, with the Egyptian boy a few paces behind.

***

The camp now resembled the scene of a massacre in some war-torn country. Bruce had known all about Egypt's troubles of course, but he hoped that, as academics, they'd avoid involvement. What was he talking about? This wasn't the work of either terrorists or government thugs. His team had been attacked by- by- Say it, Bruce, by monsters. Monsters led by a man who seemed to possess magical powers. In a rational world, it simply could not happen. But try telling that to the bodies scattered around the slowly dying fires.

A groaning from somewhere to his left alerted Bruce to the fact that not everyone had been killed. Without caution, he ran to a shuddering body on the ground. Oh God, it was Simon!

"Simon, I'm here!"

Simon stared straight ahead, as though fixated on something only he could see. "Dr Stone," he managed to say through chattering teeth. "I don't know what happened."

"I'm taking care of it, Simon, it'll be alright. Everything will be alright. Just hold on. Please."

When Simon had volunteered to load the slides for Bruce's presentation at Colombia, neither of them ever dreamed it would end here – with the promising student fighting for his life on the Egyptian sands.

Bruce knew he had to do something, but he barely trusted the authorities in these dangerous times. Luckily, there was one man who had the money to get things done right away. For the first and only time, he was glad he had Ahmed's number on speed-dial.

"It's five in the morning, Stone!" the Egyptian complained the instant he answered the call. "This better be good."

"Sir," Bruce replied, not even hesitating for a second over addressing Ahmed in a respectful fashion, "I'm going to need to you get some ambulances down here right. We have a situation."

No reply from Ahmed. Was that a good thing? Eventually, Bruce decided he couldn't wait any longer, and hung up. He started upon realising that Fusani was now standing by him.

"All this over a bracelet?" he asked the boy.

Fusani nodded. He waved a hand high in the air, signalling to Alex and Rachel that it was safe to approach.

"It's no ordinary bracelet, Dr Stone," Fusani replied.

"You don't say. I'm guessing the fact that the jewels glowed red like that when you chanted isn't ordinary either. Unless they invented the battery a lot earlier than I'd been led to believe. And that green-eyed son of a bitch? The one who killed everyone here?"

"He's not called Dr Doom. Do I have to say his name?"

"You want me to believe that was Set?"

"*The* Set?" Rachel paused in the act of dousing a fire using a canteen she'd found on the ground. Bruce wondered for a second why she didn't use her own canteen, but concluded that she was probably wise to conserve water, since none of them knew what lay ahead.

Addressing both her and Bruce, Fusani asked, "Isn't this what you expected to find here?"

"I expected to find the resting place of two extraordinary individuals, not actual Gods!" Bruce roared.

"Once the powers of Isis are activated, Set is reawakened, bent on continuing his eternal quest for her power," the boy explained. "So you see, it's not Alex's fault. Isis wanted someone to take the bracelet. Sooner or later, her battle with her brother would begin again, with the whole world as the prize. Set has been waiting for the last five thousand years for this moment. This..." he indicated the corpses, "this is only the beginning."

My God, thought Bruce, does this kid really think my daughter is Isis? Alex? My Alex?

Seemingly oblivious to Fusani's ominous prediction, Rachel observed, "So the bracelet must be the key..."

"I have questions." Everyone was surprised to hear from Alex, in spite of the fact that the situation involved her more deeply than anyone else. "This Set guy: if he's a god, why'd he run away like a total puss? Look at us – we're not exactly The Expendables here."

"Well, Set is the God of Darkness," her dad observed. "Presumably, he would either lose his powers or become significantly weaker when the sun rises. God, what am I saying?"

"Well, he's got super-speed and he controls an army of scorpion-things," Alex pointed out. "If he wants to be Set, I think we should let him be Set."

"He *is* Set," Fusani insisted. "And daylight won't be a problem for him once he gets the Bracelet of Isis."

Instinctively, Alex hugged her arm. All eyes were now fixed on her. "Whoa, OK, well, let's just give him the bracelet."

"No!" Fusani protested.

"Excuse me, it's not you he's coming after!" One more attempt to remove it failed, unsurprisingly. "OK, I'm open to suggestions. But nothing involving amputation. Except as a last resort."

"Alex, we're getting you out of Egypt tonight."

"Works for me. So how-" Her grip on her own arm tightened as a low, thrumming sound filled the air.

"Now what?" Bruce demanded, looking around for his shotgun. Damn, he thought, how could I have left it behind?

His self-recrimination was unnecessary, however, as a moment later, a helicopter appeared over the dunes. Ahmed had come through for them! Within minutes, medics were arriving in their Humvees, examining the bodies in search of survivors.

"What happened?" one asked Bruce.

What the hell to say? Best not to get into the whole giant scorpion people thing right now. Keep it simple. "Some sort of attack," he replied. "It all happened so fast. I'm not quite sure." At least that wasn't a lie. He was no longer sure of a damn thing.

Fusani certainly didn't help by observing, "It doesn't matter where you take Alex, Dr Stone, she will never be safe. Set is a god, he'll follow her anywhere. We have to stop him."

"And as an expert, Fusani, what do you suggest?" His sarcasm was entirely lost on the seventeen year-old.

"You can't stop Set," Rachel pointed out. Bruce was stunned that she was apparently completely buying into this. Then again, how could he blame her? The evidence was all around them, and it was hard to refute. While he watched the medics tending to the few survivors he tried to think it through.

"The bracelet reawakened him. Therefore..." Therefore what? What? If you really want to protect Alex, he told himself, you're going to have to go all the way, Bruce. "Therefore, there must be a way to banish him back down. Perhaps there was some clue in the tomb."

"Well, we transported all the artefacts to the lab in Cairo. Do you think one of them could hold the answer?"

"It's our only shot, Rachel. Let's go."

Alex was still uncertain. "Just to clarify, Fusani, what exactly happens, if we don't stop Set?"

"He kills you and uses the powers of Isis to plunge the world into darkness," he explained, matter-of-factly. "Unless you find a way to stop him."

"OK, so no pressure."

CHAPTER THIRTEEN

Rachel flicked on the light switches, revealing a long, all-white room. Hello, Starship Enterprise, thought Alex. The lighting in the lab was dim, in order to preserve the artefacts, she guessed. No time had been wasted in placing the items in glass cases and labelling them in multiple languages. Made sense – this discovery was a big deal, but not as big a deal as the impending conquest of the world by the God of Darkness.

The medic whose Humvee they had borrowed in order to get to the lab as quickly as possible had seemed pretty pissed at them, but only Fusani could say for certain just how pissed he really was, since all his curses had been in Egyptian, and the kid was too embarrassed to translate them. He was invaluable, however, in directing them to the lab. Traffic in Cairo was insane, much of it composed of livestock, and Fusani knew enough short-cuts to prevent any accidents.

Bruce rolled up his sleeves, probably to show that he meant business, as if stealing a medical vehicle hadn't served as sufficient proof.

In spite of the fact that they had every right to be there – scratch that, thought Alex, Rachel and my dad have every right to be here – they snuck into the building through a side entrance. Their ragged clothes didn't do a lot to inspire confidence, she figured. Indiana Jones usually looked as crappy as they did, sure, but he had the hat and the whip, too. And the backing of George Lucas.

"Alright, let's get to work," Bruce announced. "I'll begin with this row. Rachel, you take that one. Fusani, think you can manage the far row?"

Fusani nodded.

That just left Alex. "What can I do?" she asked, sheepishly.

"Try to get that bracelet off?" Bruce suggested.

Alex raised her eyebrows. "Sure, you got any butter?"

Leaving Alex to tug half-heartedly at her bracelet – really, what was the point anymore? - Bruce, Rachel, and Fusani began scrutinizing every artefact.

Half an hour later, they were halfway down their rows, and still, it seemed, no closer to discovering any clues. If Alex, who was leaning against a wall, fretting, thought they were keeping anything to themselves, her hopes were dashed when she heard her father give a loud, frustrated sigh.

"Find anything yet?" she asked him, out of a kind of mischief. He glared up at her, and she shrugged in return.

She was still watching as he glanced down half-heartedly at a case containing a jewelled stone tablet with a corner missing. His shoulders stiffened, and she knew at once that her dad was onto something.

Marching over to him as he inspected the tablet, Alex demanded, "What? What is it?"

Excitedly, Bruce rattled the glass case, only to find it locked. "Rachel, get over here. Where are the keys to these cases?"

"They're in the lab technician's office" Rachel told him. "Why, did you find something, Bruce?"

Trying to block the glare from the light on the case, he said, "I think so, but I can't quite... I need to get it out of this damn-"

Impatiently, Alex moved in front of him and grabbed the sides of the lid. Before he could protest, she ripped off the top of the case in one sharp move, bringing the lock with it. Alarm bells filled the air.

"Thank-you, Alex," Bruce drawled. "Did you know you could do that?"

"Nope. But I know now." She placed the lid carefully on the floor, even though the damage had pretty much already been done.

"You could save a fortune in bottle-openers. Now let's take a look at this..." As carelessly as her daughter had just removed the lid from the case, he pulled out the tablet and set it down on the table top.

"What are you doing?" Rachel demanded, shocked at his casual treatment of an historic artefact.

Running his finger over the tablet, Bruce announced, "I think I might have found something. You see the characters for Isis and Set?"

Frowning, Rachel nodded. The frown grew more intense as he carelessly wiped sand away with his hand.

"Bruce!"

Fusani, who had dutifully continued checking the other items, walked over to join them. "Dr Stone," he said, pointing to the door cautiously. "Someone must respond to this alarm sooner or later."

"It's OK, Fusani, we have proper clearance." No-one was reassured by this claim. If it were true, why were they being so secretive? And would security be cool with Alex's act of vandalism, no matter that it was accidental? Well, not totally accidental, but done with the best of intentions.

Before Bruce could wipe away more sand, Rachel grabbed his hand, and pulled it away from the tablet. "You are tampering with scientific research, Bruce. These artefacts need to be properly cleaned, treated with care!"

"Rachel, something out there is trying to kill my daughter," he reminded her. "Screw scientific research!"

Her jaw dropped.

At that moment, Alex couldn't think of a time when she had loved her father more.

He shook off Rachel's grip, and returned to scanning the tablet. "Here it is!"

"What's it say, Dad?"

"This is only a rough translation, but here goes: 'Whosoever wears the bracelet inherits the powers of Isis and releases the Dark God...'"

Fusani shot Alex an "I-told-you-so" look.

Having given up on dissuading him, Rachel assisted Bruce with the next section. "'When the Sun God ruled not only the sky and the earth...'"

"Oh, this'll be short," Alex interjected, sarcastically.

"'Fearful of usury, Rah created a way to make the immortal, mortal.'"

"'Mortal'?" Alex repeated. "And 'mortal' means 'killable'. That sounds promising. Go on."

"'The doomed god must be struck through the heart with the last gift of the mines of Anubis,'" Rachel read aloud.

"The last gift of the mines of Anubis obviously refers to the Knife of Horus," suggested Fusani.

Bruce smacked his head with his open palm. "Of course, I should have known!"

"Dad, there's no way we're not about to get busted for breaking and entering," Alex pointed out, anxiously. "You want to hurry it up, maybe? Where do we get this knife? Do we need a major credit card?"

"Alright, alright. Let's see..." After a few more seconds, Bruce slammed his fist down in frustration. "Dammit!"

"What? What? What does it say?"

"It doesn't say anything! Ahmed took the broken piece of the tablet. The location of the knife must be on it!"

"Oh, come on!" was the last thing Alex was able to say before a hefty, gun-toting security guard kicked open the door and began yelling at them in Egyptian.

Fusani automatically put his hands on his head. Moments later, Rachel and Alex – who may not have understood the words, but definitely got the gist of it - followed his lead. Using his free hand, the guard spoke into his microphone and the alarm finally shut off.

Slowly and carefully, Bruce produced his I.D. "Fusani," he said, "please inform him that I am Dr Bruce Stone, the leading archaeologist on this excavation. This..." he indicated the artefacts, "all belongs to me."

Fusani translated rapidly. The guard's reaction was not everything they had hoped for; he cocked his gun and aimed it directly at Bruce.

"What the hell did you tell him?" Bruce demanded.

The guard began shouting in Egyptian.

"Translate! Translate!" pleaded Alex.

"He says the police have been looking for Dr Stone. They want to ask him some questions about the massacre at the dig this morning."

Bruce nodded furiously. "Alright. Fine. Tell him I give myself up."

Alex couldn't let her dad do this. "Wait!" she cried, stepping in front of him. "This whole thing has been my fault. So you'll need to interrogate me too. Fusani, can you translate?"

Before the boy got the chance, the guard pulled a set of handcuffs from his belt and snapped them onto Alex's wrists.

"OK, I guess he understood *that*," she observed, gloomily.

As he attempted to grab Alex by the arm, she simply flexed her muscles and the cuffs snapped open again. Hey, that was easy, she thought.

The guard was too surprised to do anything affirmative with his gun, which gave Alex the opportunity to flip him bodily over a glass case, leaving him lying unconscious on the floor.

Disappointingly, Bruce did not seem particularly impressed by this latest display of her abilities. Quite the opposite, in fact. He pressed his hands to his face, despairingly.

"Oh, Jesus..." he groaned.

Fusani knelt down next to the prone guard, took the gun from his hand and slid it across the floor, out of reach.

Bruce finally got his thoughts together enough to ask, "Alex, are you seriously telling me you can break out of handcuffs, but you can't get a bracelet off?"

"I don't make the rules, Dad!" Alex protested.

"Great. Only my daughter."

Rachel, who had appeared to be in shock up until that moment, asked, "So what do we do now?"

Bruce sighed and looked back down at the tablet.

"Maybe we should pay Ahmed a visit?" Alex suggested. "I'm betting he'll be delighted to see us. Does anybody have his address?"

CHAPTER FOURTEEN

Nobody really appreciated the pressure Dr Laura Williams was under to account for every last dime the University spent. She couldn't just call Egypt whenever she wanted; the charges were really extortionate. But the news she'd just received from the Cairo police was very troubling. And Dr Stone hadn't stuck around to assist the authorities. On the contrary, he appeared to have fled the scene in a stolen vehicle. She'd neglected to mention to the Egyptian authorities that she had Bruce's cell phone number. Sooner or later, though, she'd come under pressure to give up that information, and to explain why she'd withheld it in the first place. And even she wasn't sure exactly why she'd done that. Maybe because she wanted to hear what Bruce had to say before anyone else; to judge just how bad this looked for the University. She had to know what was happening, and she'd spent too much time already trying to build up the courage to make the call. What was the time difference between the States and Egypt? Who cares – she needed answers right now. Dr Williams picked up the phone and called Bruce's number.

It was almost a full minute before he picked up.

"Dr Williams, I was actually just about to call you."

She had told herself that she would keep her patience right up until the moment he began to lie. Unfortunately, the very first thing he had said to her was clearly a lie, leaving her no option but to blow her top.

"What the hell is going on there, Bruce? I have the Cairo police calling me!"

"Yeah, we've, uh, we've had some complications."

"What do you consider a complication? Eleven people dead and five wounded?"

"Thank God!"

"What did you just say?"

"I thought almost everyone was dead! Rachel, five people made it!"

"Who are you talking to? Who else is there? I want an explanation, *Doctor*!" His attitude baffled her. He seemed distracted, as though there could possibly be anything more important than what had happened at the site.

"Where's Ahmed?" she demanded.

"Funny you should mention him. I'm about to see him right now. We're outside his house."

"Oh, yes? And did you get there in a stolen ambulance? I know all about that, Bruce."

"No, the ambulance was a little too conspicuous for downtown Cairo. We took a taxi here. I didn't get a receipt, sorry. Look, I'll definitely call you when this is all worked out."

She heard a sickening crunching sound over the line, "What the hell was that?"

"Uh, my daughter just broke something. I'll call you after I speak to Ahmed. Gotta go."

Dr Williams continued yelling for quite some time before it became clear that Bruce had hung up on her.

***

The worrying noise Laura Williams had heard moments before was, in fact, Alex Stone ripping Ahmed's door off its hinges. She had pressed the buzzer several times, but had received no answer. Frustrated, she'd been on the verge of suggesting that they go away and return another time when Rachel said, "Guess we'll have to come back later." Hearing Rachel make the same defeatist comment she had been considering enraged Alex. *If I can open a locked case and take out an armed security guard*, she figured, *why not this?* Taking a firm grip on the doorframe, she soon created a means of entry.

"Alex, I'm pretty sure that the power of Isis, if that's what this is, wasn't given to you so you could commit acts of vandalism," her father pointed out.

"You wanted to get in," Alex replied, casually flinging the door aside, "and now we're in. Come on." *Wow, that actually sounded pretty fearless*, she realised. *Joss Whedon should totally make a show about me.*

She led the way, followed by Fusani. Switching his phone off, her dad went next, motioning to Rachel to join him.

"No alarms this time," Alex observed, as they wandered from room to room, each one displaying a vulgar opulence. "Ahmed struck me as the kind of guy who cared about his security."

"She has a point, Dr Stone," Fusani said.

"We all agree she has a point, son. We're just trying not to think about what that could mean." Having checked every room on the first floor, they moved up to the next level, each one of them taking the stairs slowly and carefully.

Alex was secretly hoping that the heat of the day had got to Ahmed, and they would find him fast asleep, his snores made hideous by his crooked nose. Once they passed through a set of double doors into the study, however, she soon discovered how wrong she was (not that she'd ever seriously imagined there was much likelihood of her being correct). Paper and artefacts were strewn across the floor.

"Jesus," Bruce breathed. "The place has been ransacked!"

"Either that or he's just not too well organized," Alex suggested. "Could be the maid's day off."

Rachel called out for Ahmed, but, as expected, there was no reply. This was looking worse and worse. "Now what do we do?"

"Start searching through this mess," Bruce suggested.

As he surveyed the room with some scepticism, Fusani tensed. For a moment, Alex thought he must have been hurt during the encounter with the guard at the lab. That couldn't be, she realised, but there was definitely something up with him.

She approached, and gently put her hand in his. "What's wrong?"

"There's evil here," he said. "I can feel it."

Fusani rarely said much, but when he did, it was usually important, and always correct. If he sensed evil, then she knew it must be around somewhere. At least it couldn't be Set – the sun was still too high in the sky. Unless he'd found a way around that. He had, after all, had several thousand years to think about it.

Suddenly scared by this notion, Alex squeezed Fusani's hand. He squeezed back. This was the kind of moment she'd often fantasized about sharing with Chris. Even with the scorpions and the fate of the world in the balance, she knew instinctively that this was better.

Their hands became unclasped the moment her father, observing the exchange, cleared his throat loudly and pointedly. Without looking back, Alex headed for the bathroom. I can look for clues and pee at the same time, she thought. The door stood ajar, and as she got closer, she could see what looked like two feet wrapped in cloth. Oh, crap.

"Mr Ahmed?" she asked, knowing that whoever if it was, there was no way they would ever answer. Taking a few more steps, she saw exactly why.

"Dad..." she whispered. "There's a mummy in the bathroom."

CHAPTER FIFTEEN

Rachel dropped the desk drawer she'd been searching through. "There's a *what*?"

"A mummy," Bruce confirmed. It was indeed a human body, wrapped from head to toe in bandages.

A fat human body.

"Do you see a lot of these?" asked Alex, her voice trembling.

"Not fresh ones," he replied.

This one was, indeed, brand new. Not technically a mummy at all, Alex knew, since the drying-out process had barely begun. She was also relieved to note that there appeared to be no chance of it turning into Jet Li - not with that gut. It could be a Klingon, though; there seemed to be an odd lump around the forehead. What the hell *was* that?

Her father grabbed a knife from his belt and began cutting the cloth that covered the face.

"Maybe you shouldn't see this, honey," he suggested.

"I've already seen more dead bodies in one day than I ever thought I'd see in a lifetime," she pointed out. Anyway, she couldn't back away now even if she wanted to (which she definitely did); Fusani and Rachel were stood right behind her, watching Bruce's progress with horrified fascination.

"Gross," was all Alex had to say.

Rachel's "Oh my God!" was perhaps more appropriate.

The mummy was indeed Ahmed, his face frozen in terror. A stinger from a scorpion-man's tail was lodged in his forehead. That accounts for the bump, Alex reasoned.

Bruce felt the dead Egyptian's face. "He hasn't been dead long."

"Why would one of those monsters kill Ahmed?" Rachel wondered aloud. "I know he wasn't the nicest person, but still..."

"He had something they wanted," Fusani reminded her.

The sound of a final unbroken ornament hitting the floor and smashing indicated to the group that they were not alone. All four turned in unison to see a figure jump through a window that had been closed when they entered. Curtains billowed in the breeze.

Alex, of course, was first to reach the window. She looked down to see a scorpion-man, getting to its feet following its drop to the pavement. Looking back at her, it held up the missing piece of the tablet and smiled triumphantly. Kind of a jerk as well as a murderer, she concluded.

Pointing over Alex's shoulder at the killer, Bruce announced, "We have to catch him!" He, Fusani, and Rachel headed for the door.

If he can move as fast as his boss, Alex thought, they'll never reach him in time. Well, I'm wicked strong, so my ankles won't shatter when I land. Maybe. Oh well, no guts no glory...

Fusani looked back to see her perched on the window, preparing to jump.

"Alex!" he yelled. "No!"

Hearing the cry, Bruce rushed back into the room and grabbed his daughter's arm.

"Are you insane?" he growled.

She shook herself free of his grip; it was easier than it used to be.

"Dad, we need this," she protested, and without wasting another second thinking of all the reasons why she shouldn't jump, she jumped. A second later, she landed safely. Nothing broken, not the slightest injury. Cool. She could still see the scorpion-man, some way off. Could she still catch it? Only one way to find out...

By the time Bruce, Fusani and Rachel made it to the front door, both Alex and her quarry were out of sight.

***

If any of the people filling the Cairo streets that day had particularly sharp eyesight, they might have seen a man with a scorpion's tail followed closely by a teenage girl. More likely, though, they would have been away of being pushed aside by something that was already out of sight by the time they realised what had happened to them.

The three mortals were lagging quite a way behind in their pursuit, slowed down even further when Rachel tripped and fell.

Bruce stopped to help her up, but she simply told him, "No, you go! Go on without me! I'll be fine, go!"

He and Fusani hesitated for only a second, before leaving her and heading off in the direction they imagined Alex must have taken. Rachel pulled herself up slowly and limped after them.

***

Alex was all too aware that, thanks to her new abilities, she risked growing overconfident. She'd already experienced tremendous strength, the speed of Usain Bolt, and she was willing to bet she'd look outstanding in a bikini, but she was still far from sure what would happen when (or if) she caught up with the scorpion-man. Sure, she'd taken some Egyptian rent-a-cop with relative ease, but he was completely human. The only comfort she took was in the knowledge that this guy had already used his sting. Unless they grew back again. She wondered whether that was likely. Then she remembered she was running at warp speed, chasing after a man with a tail; she'd left "likely" behind in the States.

The light was growing dimmer as the scorpion-man took a sudden turn into an alley, jumping a chain-link fence in one bound. Not wishing to be outdone, Alex cleared the fence without difficulty, too. It was only as she landed hard on her feet on the other side that she wondered why she had suddenly stopped listening to her own words of caution.

Her eyes adjusted to the dim light, and she could make out a cloaked figure standing in the shadows, guarded by three scorpion-men. Glowing green eyes peered out at her.

Shoot, I guess it's just dark enough down here for him, she realised, backing up cautiously. What was all that stuff about overconfidence, Alex? My parents both have "Doctor" at the start of their names – how can I be so dumb? Chiding herself would have to wait, though.

Set moved closer, holding up the broken piece of the tablet. "I believe you were after this, sister?" he asked, the mockery evident in his tone.

Alex didn't know how to reply to this. I guess that's why action heroes all have scriptwriters, she thought. But she was damned if she could come up with a good comeback, so she just nodded.

Set smiled and signalled to one of the scorpion-men who stepped out from the shadows and took a challenging stance. Without even thinking, Alex knocked him down with a roundhouse kick.

Even she was surprised. Wow, I didn't even know I knew how to do that! What am I talking about, I *don't* know how to do that!

She looked up from her triumph, finally ready with a cocky comeback, to discover there was no-one around to hear it. Set was nowhere in sight. More magic? No - in the shadows, she could see that a manhole cover had been pried open. Maybe there was still time to grab him before he got away. As she prepared to leap into the sewers, it struck her that she'd blown it again. Back at the site, she'd seen Set's foot soldiers transform from scorpions into men and then back into scorpions. In the darkness, there was no way she'd spot something as small as that; not until it morphed back into human form, as happened now.

Two more scorpion-men were suddenly facing her. I am some half-assed superhero, Alex thought. When am I going to start using all of my ass? OK, this is no big problem. Just do a little Van Dammage on them, like I did on that other guy-

That other guy, meanwhile, had regained consciousness and now grabbed her around the throat. Oh, please let me be right about that sting, Alex prayed. She wasn't willing to risk it, though. She flipped her attacker over her head, slamming it on the ground. She watched it disintegrate, just like the one who'd died at the camp that morning. I'd better remember that, she thought – disintegration equals death. Just two more left to deal with. Why didn't I pick up some of Isis' armour at the lab? She obviously wore it for a reason. Yeah, because she was smart, dumbass.

With unnatural speed, she kicked the second scorpion-man, sending it tumbling to the ground. Before she could face the third goon, it had charged, and punched her in the stomach. The blow didn't hurt – not really – but it was delivered with enough force to send her reeling backwards. She knew she daren't let this freak get the better of her.

Fusani and her dad arrived at the chain-link fence just in time to witness Alex dodging the scorpion-man's punches, moving faster than seemed physically possible. She risked a glance in their direction, and saw that both guys were struggling to climb the fence. Too bad they didn't have her abilities, she thought. Even if they could get over, they probably wouldn't be to help her... not that she was doing that great herself. Her opponent's relentless punches were constantly forcing her closer to the manhole. The manhole... where Set went. OK, she decided, *you* want me to go down the manhole, *I* want me to go down the manhole. So let's get this party started.

The last thing she heard as she jumped was her dad shouting, "Alex, no! Wait!" But it was a little late for that. She just had to hope that she was able to take Set, and that the surviving scorpion-men followed her instead of deciding to stay above ground and try to take out their anger on her friends.

The most disgusting thing about jumping into a sewer wasn't the smell, although she estimated it would take at least a year to get it completely out of her nostrils, assuming she lived that long. No, it was the fact that her foot landed on a rat, which promptly exploded under the weight of her body. Not a good time for a girly freak-out, but that took some self-control, especially with the relatives of the deceased rodent scurrying around her feet. She looked around, trying to overcome the smell. Her pupils were still dilating, and she was finding it difficult to see well. Which is how she failed to spot a pair of green eyes peering at her until Set's fist hit her full in the face. She stumbled back, desperately trying to keep upright, shaking her head in shock.

"Damn, that *hurt!*" And it did. She'd grown used to nothing hurting her any more remarkably quickly. The shock at discovering that someone still had the ability to cause her pain was almost as powerful as the pain itself.

Finally her eyes adjusted, and she could see Set grinning evilly before her.

"That was some impressive fighting up above," he told her. "Now hand over the bracelet."

"And what if I don't?" She wondered if that sounded tougher to him than it did to her.

Readying her fists, she charged towards Set, who, without even flinching, grabbed her and tossed her into a wall. This was both painful *and* unsanitary.

"Okay," said Alex, climbing to her feet and checking for a nosebleed, "so you're serious."

"Always."

He was upon her immediately before she had a chance to prepare herself. She managed to get one good kick in before winding up the filthy water again. I'm not just getting my ass kicked, she realised as she crawled desperately away, I'm also going to need shots – if I even get out of here alive.

Set followed behind her, perfectly calm. "Hand over the bracelet," he repeated, "and this shall all be over."

Weakened, Alex lacked the strength to run. Bloody and beaten, she closed her eyes, bracing herself for a hit.

Set simply laughed in her face. "You always had to make things difficult, sister."

"Look, I'm sick of having to repeat myself, and I don't know what kind of freakish relationship you had with her, but I am not Isis. Besides, they've got these daytime shows now where you can work out your issues- aaagh!"

Grabbing her by her hair, Set lifted Alex off her feet.

***

Up above, things were going just as badly for Bruce and Fusani. They had given up on their attempt to scale the high chain-link fence the moment they spotted the two scorpion-men leering at them hungrily. They had begun to retreat as the creatures made it over to their side of the fence.

"What do you suggest we do now?" asked Fusani, in the same manner a person might upon learning that the movie they'd wanted to see closed yesterday.

"Run!" Bruce replied, somewhat more urgently.

They both turned and sprinted back down the alley. Bruce, of course, knew that the scorpion-men would be faster and stronger than either of them, but at that moment his survival instinct was a lot stronger than his common sense.

He felt the muscular arm one of the scorpion-men encircle his neck. Oh Christ, this is it, he thought. My death won't even be a subject of archaeological curiosity in a thousand years' time; just a dumb

American tourist who took a wrong turn and wound up getting mugged in an alley. Well, he was damned if it was all going to be for nothing; at least he could give the kid a chance to get away. Kicking frantically, he was able to reach the other scorpion-guy, who, obviously annoyed, turned his attention from Fusani. Perfect, Bruce thought. Now run, boy, run!

To his dismay, the boy didn't flee. Instead, he slid into the gap behind a dumpster. What the hell? There was no way these two monsters wouldn't find him if they really searched. Hoping to create a huge distraction, he yelled and flailed about as much as he could in the grip of the scorpion-man. The other one eyed him with amusement.

"Is that all you've got?" Bruce demanded, and that proved to be a big mistake. A massive scorpion tail rose into the air before him, and its sting plunged into his shoulder. Until that moment, the worst pain Bruce had ever known was the day he dislocated his knee tripping over one of Alex's toys when she was nine years old. But that was the equivalent of a morphine injection compared to the agony he was experiencing now. Suddenly, he felt very cold. Freezing, in fact. The chill went all the way through his body to his knees. He found he was no longer able to stand up straight. I didn't want this for Alex, he thought, not any of it. Oh, Marie, forgive me...

CHAPTER SIXTEEN

When Fusani crept slowly out from behind the dumpster a moment later, both scorpion-men were gone, and they had taken Bruce with them. They hadn't passed him, he was certain of that, and he'd been keeping an eye on the open manhole in the hope that Alex would return and use the gift of Isis to despatch their foes. The only way they could have gone, then, was over the wall. What to do? There weren't really any options. Alex had not returned, and they'd left Rachel far behind. There was no-one else but Fusani in a position to help Dr Stone, then. He did not trouble himself with the question of precisely how he was going to do that; first he had to catch up with them, then hope that some opportunity would present itself. Setting a garbage can upright, he placed it against the wall. He couldn't get over as easily as their enemies had done, but this would do just as well.

***

Tears rolled down Alex's cheeks as Set raised her into the air. Desperate to escape, she looked up, and saw immediately above her a manhole cover.

If I could get my hands on it, she thought, I could probably smash it open.

Whether Set possessed any psychic abilities, Alex didn't know, but it couldn't have been too difficult to tell what she was thinking. Before she could make her attempt, he dropped her into back into the filth yet again. So amused by her predicament was he that he permitted her time to fight her way back to her feet. As she did so, she noticed for the first time the stolen fragment of tablet in the belt round Set's waist. She tasted blood running into her mouth – at least she hoped it was blood – but for the first time since she'd landed ankle deep in a stream of crap, she felt like there was hope.

***

The Cairo streets were mobbed with Egyptians looking for a deal and tourists snapping up souvenirs. Each shop in the marketplace blasted out a different type of music- rap, hip hop, opera, classic Arabic music. The sounds jumbled together in a migraine-inducing cacophony Fusani was somehow able to disregard as he dodged dozens of traders, all of whom attempted to entice him into their shops filled with brass, jewellery and "genuine" American goods. In an attempt to avoid creating a mass panic, the two scorpion-men were now wearing cloaks, and were walking at a normal pace. Fusani was in no doubt as to their true identity – that unsightly lump under one of the cloaks could only be the prone body of Dr Stone. This was encouraging, Fusani felt. If he were dead already, they would probably have left his body where it fell. But they had taken him for a reason. Perhaps as a bargaining tool, a way of persuading Alex to part with the bracelet. Which meant, in turn, that Set didn't realise that she couldn't simply remove it when she wished. There were limits to his knowledge, it seemed. That, too, was encouraging.

Fusani's optimism left him in an instant, as a hand grabbed his arm. He whipped around to see Rachel, her finger to her lips.

***

Mustering what strength she had left, Alex charged towards Set, roaring as she went. He grinned, as she slammed into him; he didn't even stumble backwards. That seemed pretty unfair to her; even the scorpion-men had been able to knock her off her feet. But right at that moment, it didn't matter a whole hell of a lot; if anything, it just made things easier.

Swatting her away, Set roared with laughter at the sight of Alex reeling backwards, moaning, clasping one hand to her forehead. His amusement at her pain was so great that he completely failed to notice that the tablet was no longer in his belt, but in Alex's other hand.

"Oh come, come, sister, I rather enjoy fighting in the dark, don't you?"

As he moved in for the kill, Alex jumped, string the manhole with her fist, and sending it flying off. A ray of sunshine fell into the sewer. Thank Goddess, thought Alex, it's still light up top.

"Hey, asshole," she shouted, taunting him with the piece of the tablet, "try walking towards the light!"

Realised he'd been tricked, Set lunged for the tablet, ignoring the effect the light might have on him. Her strength renewed, Alex delivered a kick that sent him skidding through the filth.

"Oh, and try breathing through your nose!" she added, before leaping up into the daylight.

***

Rachel had led Fusani up a staircase at the back of a store, and now they were up on the roof, where they could better see the two scorpion-men carrying Dr Stone away. Following from above was certainly more convenient, Fusani realised, since it took them away from the insanity of the market, but he wondered whether she'd considered just how they were going to get back down in a hurry.

And it looked as though they were going to have to get down immediately. There was a huge commotion holding up traffic on the main street. Fusani and Rachel craned their necks, but it was hard to tell exactly what had just happened; shoppers were crowding round the event, straining to get a view.

The scorpion-men, too, had been stopped in the traffic. There was never going to be a better chance than this to catch them.

Motioning to Rachel, Fusani cried, "Come on! Now!"

Rachel shook her head, furiously. Afraid, probably. And he couldn't blame her. He would undoubtedly be terrified if he thought about it for even a second. But Alex hadn't shown any fear when she went after Set. How could he do any less for her father? He just hoped that the canopy below him wouldn't rip as soon as he jumped onto it. There was, mercifully, enough spring in it to propel him onto the back of the scorpion-man who held Dr Stone. A moment later, Rachel followed, tackling the other one. There was no way either of them possessed the strength to overpower one of Set's creations, but the fact that they were packed in by onlookers might alter the odds, even if only slightly. Fusani doubted that the punch he delivered caused his scorpion-man any pain, but in reacting, the creature tripped over several pairs of feet, losing its grip on Dr Stone at the same time.

Rachel quickly abandoned her foe, and rushed to where Bruce lay on the ground.

"Bruce," she called, grabbing him by the chin and shaking his head, "can you hear me? Wake up!"

A groan was all she got by way of reply, but Fusani heard it, too. So he *was* alive.

Before the scorpion-men could retrieve their captive, the source of the commotion became clear.

A teenage girl had emerged from the sewers, having somehow punched a manhole cover into the path of oncoming traffic, resulting in a near-collision of vehicles, and several startled donkeys.

The crowds were, naturally, horrified, at the sight of a person dripping with stuff they'd hoped they'd seen the last of in their hotel bathrooms, but Fusani thought he'd never seen anything so magnificent in his entire life. His appreciation of this sight was cut suddenly short by a massive scorpion tail, which plunged into the ground perilously close to where he stood.

People were only too happy to make way for Alex as she stumbled through the crowd, bruised, bloody and filthy.

"Let me tell you..." she said breathlessly, "you haven't experienced Egypt until you've seen it from under-"

All of a sudden, something up ahead caught her eye. Fusani? No way! But it *was* Fusani, and he was fighting with a scorpion-man! And Rachel, Rachel was trying to wrench the prone figure of her dad away from another one of Set's warriors. Whatever had been done to her dad, it gave her renewed strength. She pushed her way through the few onlookers whose sense of smell hadn't already told them to back off, and tackled the big-tailed bastard who was trying to grab her father. A single punch sent it to the ground. Round One to Alex.

Rachel was able to drag Bruce away to safety, as Alex wailed mercilessly on the other scorpion guy. She'd pretty much used up the last of her strength, and still it was only on its knees. But on its knees, and unable to stand up, which meant that things were still going her way. She managed one final kick to the face, which was all that was needed to start the process of disintegration.

Alex: Two, Forces of the Underworld: Squat. Hope Set didn't have any money on the outcome, she thought. Then she changed her mind, and kind of hoped he did.

Seeing that Alex had knocked all the fight out of the remaining scorpion-man, Fusani delivered one final punch, turning it to dust. Awestruck tourists began reaching for their camera-phones.

Rachel assisted Bruce and Fusani did the same for Alex; with as much speed as they could manage, they carried both members of the Stone family to the edge of the market place. Bruce raised his hand, and mumbled.

"What? What is it, Bruce?" Rachel pleaded.

"He's pointing to that," said Fusani.

An open-top double-decker bus, which Alex imagined, looked about as badly beaten up as she probably did, was approaching. Flagging the vehicle down, all four climbed aboard. Passengers eyed the bloody and dirty group, as they made their way to the back. Fusani greeted everyone, as though there was nothing remotely odd about their appearance whatsoever, before helping Alex into the seat by the window, where she could rest next to her father, and catch her breath.

"I can honestly say I never saw any of this coming," she said, before passing out for a couple of minutes.

CHAPTER SEVENTEEN

Alex's head was still swimming as she came round. She wasn't sure what had happened to her dad, but he looked in pretty bad shape. And why did Fusani refuse to take his eyes off her? Maybe he couldn't believe how lousy she looked. She'd been humiliated many times in her short life, but even before her Isis makeover, she'd never been covered in sh-

"Whoa."

Now she knew what he was looking at. She held her hands out and watched in amazement as her cuts slowly began to heal.

"You should have waited for us," said her dad, wearily. He was fully conscious at last. "You're not as strong in places like that."

"Brought you back a souvenir," Alex grinned, handing him the tablet.

"That's my girl." He tried to concentrate on deciphering the hieroglyphics, but couldn't help wincing when Rachel opened his shirt to examine the wound on his shoulder.

"Oh my God!" Alex exclaimed. "You got stang!"

"'Stung', honey. It's pronounced 'stung.'"

At least he was well enough to correct her grammar. That's got to be a good sign, she thought.

"Wow, they really got you good," observed Rachel. "What about you, Alex, are you alright?"

"I'm fine," she snapped, even though that obviously wasn't true.

"Are you sure. honey? That cut on your forehead looks pretty deep, and it hasn't healed like the others."

For some reason, calling her "honey", only made Alex want to deny any infirmity with greater vehemence. "I'm *fine*," she insisted.

Becoming more alert all the time. Bruce motioned to Rachel's canteen. "Can I have some of your water?"

Rachel shrugged. "Sorry, it's empty. What about the tablet? Was it worth it, Bruce? Where are we headed?"

"According to the missing fragment, Luxor Island."

"Never heard of it," said Alex, wanting to be involved in some positive way.

"That's about eighty miles down the Nile," Fusani volunteered, perking up at the news.

Bruce nodded, resting his head against the window. "Uh-huh. It makes sense. Alex's mother and I excavated a Sethian temple there almost twenty years ago. Hopefully, I still have the map. I packed pretty much everything when I knew I was coming here."

Alex considered the notion of an entire island dedicated to Set, kicker of seventeen year-old asses and would-be conqueror of the world. Great.

"This is perfect!" Fusani observed, without, as usual, a trace of irony. "The bus will stop at the docks."

"Perfect," she agreed, with a huge trace of irony. "But do you think I could take a shower at some point?"

Her father looked her up and down. "Yes, I believe that is our first priority."

For what felt like the first time in a million years, each one on them was able to manage a smile. But Alex saw that her dad's vanished quickly, replaced by a look of shock. She turned her head to see what had freaked him out, and found herself looking straight into the leering face of another scorpion-man.

It was clinging to the outside of the bus, glaring in at them. The other bus passengers began to panic, and the reason soon became clear – all the windows were covered with the creatures.

"Oh God, they found us!" Rachel wailed.

Alex was frozen to the spot. One of the scorpion-men was trying to pry open the emergency exit door. If it succeeded, the entire bus would be swarming with those things, and there was no way she could fight them all off. She wondered why the driver didn't stop. Was he aware his bus was under attack, or did he just think he had some incredibly rowdy passengers?

"Time to get off," Alex suggested. They began heading for the front of the bus, just as the scorpion-man succeeded in ripping off the emergency door. Six more of its brothers joined it inside. If the passengers had been scared before, they went insane with fear now. The ensuing chaos gave them a chance to flee up the stairs, Fusani supporting Bruce all the way.

There was no way the tourists on the upper level of the bus couldn't have heard what was going on below, but none of them was crazy enough to go down and see what all the commotion was about. It was enough of a shock when Alex and her group suddenly appeared, heading for the back of the bus. With their ragged clothes and desperate expressions, it would have been easy to think they were the cause of the distress; actually, Alex considered, glancing at Isis' bracelet, I guess I kind of am.

Watching traffic zooming by on either side, she weighed up their options. At least, she would have liked to, but there didn't seem to be any way off the bus that didn't involve winding up as a bloody smear in the road.

"We have visitors," Fusani noted, calmly.

A scream from one of the tourists alerted them to the presence of a scorpion-man at the top of the stairs. It spotted them and shrieked - a signal to the others, Alex guessed.

What could she do? In a second, this level would be crawling with scorpion-men, attacking her friends and finishing off her already-wounded father. She took one last hopeless look over the side of the bus. Wait a second, she thought, maybe not so hopeless. Not if we act fast.

"Come on," she yelled at the others, "we have to jump!"

Her father shook his head. "I don't think so, Alex. Out of a building is one thing, but off a speeding bus?"

"Dad, it's the only way!"

Rachel, too, seemed unconvinced. "If you're so sure, you jump first!" she said.

Oh well, at least she's treating me like an adult, Alex thought. That's a good thing, I guess. Well, if she wants to get tough with someone who possesses the power of a goddess, fine. Let's see how that works out for her.

Ignoring Rachel's vociferous protests, Alex simply picked her up and tossed her over the side. Bruce cried out in alarm, as he and Fusani looked down to see that Rachel had landed safely in the bed of a truck carrying Egyptian cotton. She seemed to be completely fine which, Alex was ashamed to note, irritated her slightly.

More scorpion-men were emerging from the staircase. They had seconds left, if they were going to get away. There was no more time to think it through.

"Jump, or I'll throw you!" Alex told the guys. "But decide now!"

"Oh dear God," breathed Bruce as he closed his eyes, and jumped off the side. Alex and Fusani followed close behind.

By the time the scorpion-men made it to the spot they had all leapt from, there was no sign of them – only an apparently empty cotton truck, speeding ahead of them.

***

Alex unearthed herself from the pile of cotton, gasping for breath. Was there any substance she wasn't going to wind up covered in?

Fusani and Rachel surfaced, both of them pulling threads from their mouths. All three looked about for Bruce. There was no sign of him.

"Dad?"

Alex began to panic. She hadn't actually seen him land on the truck before she and Fusani jumped. Oh God, please don't say he'd missed. There was no way he could survive a fall from a fast-moving bus – he'd tried to warn her. What had she done? She'd tried to protect him and instead she'd ended up killing him.

A dull moan came from the depths of the cotton. Alex thrust a fist into the middle of it, and pulled up her father, cotton sticking to his sweaty face. Even he couldn't help smiling, just a little.

Singing along to his radio, the driver of the truck was clueless as to what had just happened. A movement in the rear-view mirror suddenly caught his eye. He turned and was startled to see Fusani, who had crawled towards the cabin of the truck and was now leaning through the driver's window.

"Could you take us to the docks, please?"

Confused and still shaking from the scare, the driver nodded.

CHAPTER EIGHTEEN

"Hey! There's a line, in case you hadn't noticed."

As a matter of fact, Bruce had seen the line; it was about a mile long, and made up of tourists waiting to organize their boat trip with the guy in the booth. But the end of the world as we know it couldn't wait, so he, Alex, Fusani and Rachel weaved through the crowds to get to the front of the line, oblivious of the glares from other tourists.

A tubby bespectacled Englishman wearing a T-shirt about a size too small, leaned towards his improbably attractive wife and muttered, "Probably American."

In the past, Alex would have been embarrassed beyond belief by something like this, but right now, she was past caring. That jerk had no idea. The only other person in the world who could have understood what she was going through was Percy Jackson, and he was fictional.

His breathing still laboured from the scorpion bite, Bruce said to the shrunken man in the booth, "I need a boat to Luxor Island."

The man pointed to the long line. "We don't travel to that island," he croaked. "No-one does. Next."

He motioned for the next tourist to step forward, but Bruce blocked the window. "Look, it's imperative that we get there as soon as possible!" he insisted.

"What makes you think I would care?"

That was a point it was almost impossible to dispute; but Bruce thought he just might have a persuasive argument. It always seemed to work in the movies when someone presented a handful of bills as a bribe. He'd learned to always carry an emergency cash stash. Reaching into his wallet, Bruce laid five hundred dollars on the counter.

"That's American currency," he pointed out, hoping that the exchange rate was good. These days, who knew?

For a second, Bruce thought it was actually going to work, with the man in the booth eyeing the money hungrily. Then the second passed, and he slowly shook his head.

"Not for all the money in the world would I travel there. No-one in their right mind would go to Luxor Island. That place is evil. Next."

Making sure he snatched up all his notes, Bruce stalked away, taking a second to apologise to the English couple, who were tutting furiously.

"Now what?" asked Rachel.

Bruce looked back to the docks. Beautiful white boats lined the small harbour, gently bobbing in the water. Strong, strapping, seaworthy captains ordered their crews around the decks. So near, and yet so far.

"He said no-one in their right mind goes to Luxor Island," he reported.

"So?" asked Alex.

"Maybe we ask someone who isn't," Fusani suggested.

"Isn't what?"

"In their right mind."

There was a smaller vessel was tied to the docks at the end of the pier. Paint so dirty it was impossible to tell its original colour chipped away on the hull, and it looked as though no-one was actually on the boat. A deserted boat. Not in the best condition, but it was floating, kind of. Obviously, nobody wants it, Bruce thought. It wouldn't really be stealing, he supposed.

"You know..." he said at last, "we could always just-"

As they got closer to the boat, they heard sounds of life. Sounds of sleeping life. Closer still, and they saw what Bruce imagined must be the captain, dozing in a deckchair, the newspaper over his face moving up and down in time with his snores.

"We could always just what?" Fusani asked, loudly.

"Never mind." Attempting to wake the captain, Bruce cleared his throat. Nothing. He tried again.

Still nothing.

"I don't think there's anything we can do," Rachel noted.

Alex whistled loudly - so loudly that the captain nearly fell out of his chair.

Ripping the newspaper from his face, Bruce saw that he appeared to be about seventy, tufts of grey hair sticking out from the sides of his hat, and larger tufts sticking out from both ears. He eyed the four of them suspiciously.

Alex gave him a cheerful wave in return.

"What do you want?" he asked.

Bruce took another step forward. "We'd like to, uh, hire your boat," he said, trying to erase from his mind the fact that just a few seconds earlier, he had considered stealing the craft.

"Hire the *Nefertiti*?"

"Yes, please," said Rachel. "For you to take us to Luxor Island."

"For five hundred dollars," Bruce added, quickly

The captain considered this for a moment. "Luxor, huh? No-one goes there, you know."

"So we heard," responded Rachel.

"It's very important," Alex assured him.

He looked at her, as if she'd just popped out of nowhere. Bruce decided to gets his attention back by waving the money in front of his face.

"Five hundred, you say?"

"Uh-huh," Bruce answered. "American currency"

The old man glanced down the pier at all the beautiful boats. "You already asked them?"

"They won't help us."

Nobody spoke for a long time. The captain might have been thinking it over. Or, he might have been about to fall asleep standing up. So far as Bruce could tell, it was about about fifty-fifty. At last, the old man gave them all a wide, largely toothless grin.

"Well," he said, "I always did enjoy challenging death."

Bruce turned to face his party. "Good news, guys..."

The looks on their faces did not suggest they considered it good news.

CHAPTER NINETEEN

Alex had imagined that it would take a million showers before she would ever feel clean again, but the one in her cabin on board the *Nefertiti* did the job pretty well. The plumbing looked as ancient as everything else on board (including the captain, who still hadn't given them his name – tax problems, she guessed), but it seemed to do the job. She didn't exactly step out of the shower feeling like a new woman – face it, thanks to the bracelet of Isis, she already *was* a new woman – but she felt like she had successfully sent the last of the Cairo sewers down the drain, and that was good enough.

Examining herself in a grimy mirror, she noticed that her swollen lip was finally back to normal. Thanks, Isis, she thought; this is really going to cut down on my time spent with the school nurse after soccer practice. Additionally, she could see no sign of the cut on her forehead that Rachel had mentioned earlier. Maybe she had been kind of hard on Rachel; she was only showing her concern. And for that, she recalled, I threw her off a moving bus. Shame on me. Is that some side-effect of the bracelet? No. No, it's all me.

A knock on the door brought Alex back to the here and now.

"Coming!" she yelled. "Hold on!" Grabbing a complimentary but un-laundered robe from the closet, she opened the door to discover Fusani, another silly grin plastered all over his face.

"What's up?" he asked.

"I... What *is* up?" she responded, for a lack of anything more intelligent to say.

"I just wanted to see how your battle wounds were."

She smiled sheepishly. "They're fine."

"*So* fine."

She wondered whether that meant the same in Egypt as it did back in the States. Not that anyone outside of an '80s TV rerun still described a person that way. Maybe they're just getting out old shows, she imagined. Alex knew that was total garbage, but she felt uncomfortable focusing on the fact that as Fusani stepped forward, he brushed her hair aside to feel where the cut had been.

"It's like it was never there," he whispered. She could feel his breath. Oh God, that feels good. Better than any A.C. "That's amazing."

"Uh-huh," she agreed. She wasn't a hundred per-cent sure what she was agreeing to, but she didn't much care. He was so close, she could practically breathe him in. If there was ever a perfect moment for a first kiss – for a first *everything* – this was it. She closed her eyes, bit her lip and savoured the moment.

She must have savoured it for too long, because when she opened her eyes again, Fusani was back in the doorway again. Oh God, what had she done wrong? Had she been too slutty? Or not slutty enough? She looked to the ground, feeling her cheeks burning with embarrassment.

But whatever Fusani was feeling at the moment, it wasn't embarrassment. He moved closer again, leaning down to make eye contact with her.

"I believe you're blushing, Isis," he said.

"I am not!" she lied, fighting the urge to break out into a smile that would outdo his for sheer gleeful goofiness.

He put his hand on her cheek. It felt cool - a sexy, foreign kind of coolness.

"Your face is warm."

She pushed his hand away - playfully, she hoped. "Stop it!"

"I didn't think goddesses blushed."

"Oh yeah? How many do you know?"

Fusani grinned. "Just one, apparently."

She rocked from side to side, coquettishly. "And sometimes, she blushes."

"Point taken. Alright, I'm going to have a word with the captain. Find out how long we're on here."

He gave the cutest wave as he walked off down the corridor.

Alex shut the door and leaned against it, grinning like a crazy person. Now she knew he was totally into her - she really didn't have to worry...

***

...Except about the troupe of Scorpion-men who moved stealthily along the banks of the Nile, tracking the Nefertiti.

Had Bruce and Rachel, who were, at that moment, reclining on chairs at the back of the boat, been more alert, they might have noticed several pairs of golden eyes, glowing in the brush. But their thoughts were elsewhere. Bruce's were primarily about how good Rachel was looking that evening. Since the discovery of the Tomb of the Gods, there'd been no time to think about that sort of thing. But now, while technically still racing against time, they had the opportunity to sit and relax for a while.

"Mmm... Now this is more like it," she purred.

"I couldn't agree more," he said, closing his eyes. "I must say, I did not expect this turn of events."

"Which part?" she asked. "The part where Set rises from the dead or the part where your daughter turns out to be the reincarnation of a goddess?"

Bruce chuckled. "I don't know whether you'd exactly call her a reincarnation, but... Pretty much all of it, yeah."

"Me neither."

"It's amazing, isn't it? That this is actually happening. I've been researching Egyptian mythology all my life, but I never thought..." He ran out of words, looking into Rachel's eyes. She was staring tenderly back at him. It was obvious there was something on her mind.

"Bruce," she said at last, "there's something I..."

Whatever was on her mind right then, it failed her at the last moment.

"Never mind. So, when was the last time you were at Luxor Island? Twenty years ago, you said?"

"Probably more like eighteen. It was our first dig after we were married, Marie and me. It was the rainy season, and the Nile flooded. We were up to our knees in water every day."

"What awful conditions," she said, but Bruce seemed to think he caught something in her voice that suggested she wasn't that concerned.

"Somehow we didn't seem to mind."

"And what did you discover? Was there anything in the temple?"

He shook his head. "Funding fell through. National Geographic was planning on using the temple for their *Ancient Mysteries of Egypt* show. But after two months, with camera crews everywhere, the execs felt we hadn't discovered anything captivating enough, and we were forced to abandon the project."

Funding problems, he thought. The bane of every archaeologist. Back then, it was down to ratings. This time, it had all been in the lap of a fat Egyptian businessman who had wound up mummified in his own bathroom. Bruce definitely hadn't seen that coming. Neither had Ahmed, he bet.

"When did she pass away?" Rachel asked.

"In nine days, it will have been a year." He hadn't circled it on his calendar, but he knew it instinctively, even when it wasn't at the front of his mind. "She was so strong, even to the end," he recalled.

"It must have been so hard for Alex. Now's the time a girl needs her mom the most."

Bruce was glad Rachel took an interest in Alex's well-being, but she raised a point that hadn't really occurred to him.

"Do you think?"

Rachel puts her hand on his. It felt nice. It felt right.

CHAPTER TWENTY

Alex was asleep in her bed when the door to her cabin opened. A pair of green eyes calmly examined the figure of the young girl, curled up in a ball under the covers, one arm hanging over the side of the bed. And wrapped round that arm, a distinctive bracelet.

Slowly, Set slid into the room, approaching Alex's bed. Reaching out for her, his fingers gently wrapping not around her arm, but her neck. He smiled with satisfaction as he began to squeeze...

Alex sat up in horror, gasping for breath. Oh wow. She'd never been so relieved to wake from a dream, never. A while ago, the most terrifying thing that had ever happened to her in her bedroom was the discovery of a really wicked-looking spider. Now she was having hallucinations about being strangled by an ancient Egyptian god with a thing for scorpions. Not a good time to be alone.

***

Fusani was leaning over the *Nefertiti*'s railing, staring out into the river. Alex had no idea what was going on in his mind, but then, she never did. Somehow he sensed her presence before she even spoke.

"The captain says we'll be at Luxor Island by early morning," he said.

"Uh-huh. Did you find out his name yet?"

"I didn't think it polite to ask."

She joined the young Egyptian at the railing.

"Fusani, I never got to thank you..."

He laughed. "Thank me for what?"

"You know, for saving my dad, for coming with us on this nightmare."

"It's not like I had any other plans."

Was it her imagination, or did she just see a flash of gold over there on the bank? No, of course not. That crazy dream was still preying on her mind.

"Your family would be worried if they knew," she told him.

"No they wouldn't. As long as I give them part of my earnings, they don't care where I go."

She'd rarely heard Fusani talk seriously about anything before. What was she to say?

"I'm sure that's not true."

"You don't know them."

OK, he'd got her there.

"Alex, I understand you have some problems with your father, but Dr Stone is a good man."

He was right. She knew he was right. But knowing it and admitting it were two different things.

"So what do you do when you're not helping Americans kill off Egyptian gods?" she asked. "What do you and your friends do for fun?"

"I'm kind of a loner," he replied.

"Yeah, I can see that."

Fusani raised his eyebrows. "Thanks."

Was he joking, or had she hurt his feelings? Why was this guy so difficult to read?

"Oh, I- I didn't mean anything like- I'll just stop talking."

He laughed, and it was adorable. Adorable and just a little frustrating.

"Please, Alex, don't ever stop," he said.

And she might not have done, had she not been distracted by the sound of her father's raised voice, as he emerged from his cabin.

***

Foolishly, Bruce had switched his cell back on in order to check his messages, and within seconds, it had begun to ring. Even more foolishly, he had chosen to answer it.

Dr Williams was not really interested in his attempts to explain recent developments, particularly since this mostly involved avoiding specific details, such as scorpion-men, the resurrected Set and the forthcoming enslavement of the human race. Even he found it pretty hard to take, and he'd been a witness to it; hearing it all over the phone, it would definitely sound like he'd succeeded in locating some high-grade pot instead of ancient artefacts.

"I realize this puts you in an awkward position," he told Williams, "but I really have no idea who murdered Ahmed." OK, not strictly true, but it was another of those instances where the truth was really too much to bear.

Alerted by the tension in his voice, Rachel came out of her own cabin. Spotting her, Bruce motioned her to join him. A roll of his eyes was all it took to convey who was on the other end of the line.

"Well the Cairo police seem to think they have a suspect," said Williams. "My lead archaeologist, who told me he was just about to speak to Ahmed minutes before he was discovered dead."

"You are certainly not suggesting-" Bruce didn't feel like going on. He was guessing the cops hadn't told her anything about the body being mummified when they found it, or even about the sting embedded in his head. Instead, he said, "Listen, Dr Williams, my daughter is in danger!" He rubbed his shoulder – the damn thing still ached, and it only got worse the more stress he was under. While he ignored Williams, Rachel inspected his scorpion wound. It still hurt like hell, but something felt better.

"This is your career, Bruce," Williams continued. "I'm sure your daughter can wait a day or two. She has before. Now listen to me very carefully. You've embarrassed me and the board and ruined Colombia's reputation."

Bruce winced, not at the pain in his shoulder, but at Dr William's severity.

"Bruce, if you return to Cairo now for a debriefing, I may be able to save your reputation."

He thought about for a moment, but he knew there was really no need. "Thanks for the kind offer, Dr Williams, but I think I'll just stay here and save my daughter."

Before she could make her inevitable protest, he tossed the phone over the side of the boat. He looked triumphantly at Rachel.

"Oh my God, Bruce," she breathed, in a tone that could only mean "I am so hot for you right now."

She wrapped her arms around him, and even though that meant she was pressing her body against his wound, that was OK with him.

"I think I just got fired," he explained, although that outcome must surely have been pretty obvious.

"I guess so. Sorry, Bruce."

"Meh. I'll take being alive any day."

"I really admire you, you know." Before he could say thanks, she went on, looking deep into his eyes as she spoke. "I admire your intelligence, your bravery, your sensitivity..."

It was probably time to say something appropriate, Bruce reasoned, but the opening of his mouth to speak provided her with an opportunity to kiss him. It was the first time he'd been kissed since Marie, and there hadn't been too many women before her. Whatever he'd been planning to say, he could no longer remember it. He couldn't think of anything much, or to notice anything, even his own daughter, who had been heading towards him beaming, and whose mouth dropped at the sight of him locking lips with Rachel.

As Alex's eyes welled up with tears, she brushed past Fusani, heading back down the deck to her cabin. The young Egyptian went after her, pausing only for a second when he thought he spotted something moving along the banks of the river. Something... golden.

It was deeply unfortunate that Alex hadn't stuck around, or she would have seen her father pull back from Rachel, as though experiencing a jolt from a live electrical cable. Whatever he originally planned to say, it was long gone, but he knew now what he had to say.

"Rachel... I chose you as my assistant because of your qualifications. And while I'm deeply flattered that your feelings for me go beyond work... I'm afraid mine do not."

Rachel said nothing. She simply returned to her cabin, leaving Bruce alone. Again.

CHAPTER TWENTY-ONE

Its evil reputation notwithstanding, Alex figured that the appearance of Luxor Island would be enough to keep tourists away. It wasn't that it was in the shape of a skull, or anything; it just looked like something the ocean had coughed up.

The aged captain of the *Nefertiti* seemed perfectly capable of overlooking its shortcomings, however.

"There she is, my friends," he announced, proudly, like he was showing off his kid's soccer trophies.

Fusani moved to the railing to get a better look.

"Now, there's no area for me to dock safely," the captain went on, "so I'll just have to let you off close by."

"Excuse me?" said Bruce, flabbergasted. "Let us off? I thought we had an arrangement."

"We did. I said I'd take you to Luxor Island. I never said I'd wait for you."

It was Alex's turn to weigh in. "Are you kidding me? So what was all the crap about challenging death you gave us back at the docks?"

The captain appeared unmoved. "I can challenge it perfectly well from here."

"This is terrific! What, so you're just going to leave us stranded?"

"I'll come back for you before sunset. You have my word."

"We had your word that you'd take us to the island."

By way of reply, the captain simply held out his arm, indicating the hideous rock before them. Take it or leave it.

Not even Alex knew what they ought to do at that moment. Pissed as she still was at her dad for the "Rachel Incident" of the night before, she looked to him now for a decision. Looking to someone for a decision while stubbornly refusing to make eye contact was, she discovered, really hard.

"There really isn't any other choice," he pointed out. "The Knife of Horus is on that island, maybe. And it's the only thing that can kill Set. We have to try."

Though she knew he was absolutely right, Alex couldn't help making a scoffing noise and turning her back on her bemused father.

***

Alex, Bruce, Rachel and Fusani all paused to watch the *Nefertiti* turn north as they trudged through the shallow water.

"He's so going to leave us," Alex predicted.

Her father simply shook his head in confusion. That's right, thought Alex, act like nothing happened. But you know what happened. And I know.

"Just what did you expect me to do, Alex?" he enquired, sharply.

"I wouldn't expect anything from you," she said, and marched on ahead to the shoreline.

Once they were all on solid ground, Bruce opened his pack and pulled out his map of the island. Alex was slightly embarrassed upon noticing the hole she'd made in it earlier with her super-sneeze.

"If I remember correctly," her dad said, "the temple ruins are located on the south-east side of the island."

"And that would be just super, if we knew which side of the island we were on right now," Alex added, unhelpfully. Wow, she thought, I'm really kind of a bitch today.

Silently, Rachel produced a compass from her pocket and passed it to Bruce. Looking over his shoulder, Fusani noted what the compass said, looked to the position of the sun, then pointed in the direction they needed to go.

Bruce smiled up at him. "Impressive, kid."

"Where'd you learn that?" Rachel asked.

Fusani simply smiled in reply.

Terrific, thought Alex. I'm the one with super powers, and everyone else is making me look like crap. No, she realised, as the party headed into the brush, *I'm* the one who's making me look like crap. But that still didn't change the way she felt about her dad at that moment.

She and Fusani lagged behind as Bruce led the way through the dense foliage. Rachel, of course, followed him closely. Alex noticed that they were talking in low tones. About their wedding, maybe. Not about getting rid of her by sending her to a boarding school, she knew that much; her dad had taken care of that already. She kicked a rock in frustration, and watched as it sailed off into the distance.

Not only was she irritated by her father's behaviour, she was now physically irritated, too. A fern branch was scratching at the back of her neck. She swatted at it absent-mindedly. OK, now she was mad. Alex grabbed the branch and yanked it forward, only to have Fusani – who was attempting to tease her out of her crappy mood by tickling her with a fern branch – collide with her. She whipped around, annoyed, but the boy simply smiled at her - that gorgeous, unreadable smile.

Refusing to be cheered up by him, she turned back to ensure that her father wasn't getting up to anything with Rachel. And that was the moment she realised they were both gone. But not far - she and Fusani found them in a nearby clearing, where they'd come to a sudden halt. And now Alex could see why – Rachel and Bruce were staring at the ruins, ancient stones put together with perfect precision. Creeper vines had consumed most of what was left of the walls, but she could imagine how beautiful it must have been. Had Isis ever been here, she wondered? Was this where she and Set had their final battle? If so, why couldn't Alex remember it? She had all of Isis' powers, but none of her memories, and none of the experience that might help her to use those powers better.

Ignoring the outer walls, her father made for a shallow doorway at the far wall, Rachel following obediently after him.

Alex and Fusani moved more slowly, taking it all in.

"If I remember correctly," Bruce said, "the first set of hieroglyphics was right inside the doorway." He pulled out a flashlight and clicked it on, illuminating the small room within. It seemed kind of cramped to Alex.

"This is it?" Rachel asked. "The Temple of Set?"

He nodded, entering the ruin without caution. Alex flinched, expecting lethal darts to strike him at any moment. But the booby-trap makers must have been out of town when this place was built. Without any of his daughter's apprehension, Bruce knelt and brushed away the dirt from the walls with his palms. Rachel joined him, and they began reading the hieroglyphics carved into the wall. Fusani, too, got to work on the inscriptions covering the opposite side of the room.

Which leaves me, as usual, with nothing to do but stand in the doorway with an expression of slack-jawed amazement on my face, thought Alex.

"How old is this temple?" she asked, wanting be a part of things in some way.

After mumbling a quick calculation, her dad replied, "About three-and-a-half thousand years."

"Wow."

Five minutes later, every wall had been translated. And it seemed from the archaeologists' expressions, that it hadn't helped one bit.

"I don't believe it," Bruce groaned. "Not one word about the Knife of Horus! Not-one-word! We came all this way for nothing."

"Is there another temple?" asked Rachel.

"No," he replied, bitterly. "I've been here before. Trust me, this is it."

"So now what?" Alex wondered.

"I'm not quite sure."

Bruce looked and sounded beaten. Rachel patted his arm, supportively.

Alex couldn't help herself. "Well, at least someone's enjoying this trip," she said, acid in every word.

"Alex, I really don't have time for this right now," Bruce snapped.

Frustrated by his attitude, she emitted a sigh so powerful, it created a small dust swirl.

"Fine, I'll just go play out there in the jungle till you guys are done. I'll tell Predator you said hi."

Alex noticed that Rachel hadn't said a word about all this. Standing by her man, maybe? She failed to noticed, that Fusani, too, was silent during the exchange. But he was always pretty quiet, so it was easy to take him for granted.

"Your sarcasm is not appreciated," Bruce told his daughter. "I guess Rachel and I are the only ones who realize just how grave the situation is."

Visibly upset, Alex simply said, "Yeah, you guys make a great team."

Bruce stared hard at her, but if he was attempting to read her, it only irritated her more. He should have known what was upsetting her without her needing to spell it out for him.

Finally, Rachel spoke, but not to defend Bruce. "I'm going to examine the outside of the temple. Maybe there's a clue we've overlooked out there."

Good call, Alex thought. Just keep on walking, and don't stop when you reach the shore. She didn't watch Rachel leave, just kept looking straight ahead. But she also wanted Rachel to know she wasn't watching. Unfortunately, she couldn't turn round to see Rachel watching her *not* watching, so how could she be certain? Wow, being a Class-A bitch was complicated.

"Fusani, could you help me?" was the last thing she heard Rachel say.

The boy looked to Alex, but she was too mad to speak, and couldn't think what to say anyway, so he followed Rachel out a moment later.

"Alex, what is going on?" asked her dad in frustration. "Why all this anger?"

Tears clouded her eyes, but the scowl remained on her face. "I saw you, Dad."

"You saw me? You saw me where? Doing what? What are you talking about?"

Alex had never realised what a good liar her dad was. She could almost believe he hadn't done anything, if she hadn't seen it with her own eyes.

"Last night on the back deck..." she began, her voice at risk of breaking up.

"What?" he demanded.

"I saw you two kiss."

Her father's sigh didn't create a mini-tornado like Alex's had done, but it was filled with as much emotion.

"It was a momentary lapse of judgement," he said.

Like that explains everything, Alex thought. Unbelievable!

"My feelings for Rachel do not extend past the purely professional."

"Oh yeah, right!" she responded. Not the snappiest comeback in the world, she knew, but it adequately conveyed her disbelief.

"I'm telling the truth. I wouldn't lie to you, Alex."

Liar, she thought.

"I'll be honest, there was a while when I wondered... But I couldn't do it. Look, honey, it was just a kiss, that's all."

To someone who, at seventeen years old, was still waiting for her first kiss, this didn't sound to Alex like the small deal her father seemed to think it was.

"Even if it was 'just a kiss', how could you do that to mom? Don't you miss her at all?"

He didn't answer straight away. "Every day."

"Well you sure don't act like it."

"Showing my grief wouldn't solve anything."

Alex felt like she wanted to punch something. "That's always it with you, isn't it, Dad? It's always about trying to fix something! Can't you just let your feelings show without coming up with a- a scientific explanation for them?"

"Now, you're simply not making sense."

Now she felt like she wanted to scream *and* punch something. "Sometimes not making sense is OK, Dad!"

"That's not who I am, Alex."

"Well that *is* who *I* am. And mom would have understood that. I wish she were here." Then, because she felt she hadn't quite made her point, she added, "*She* would have found the knife."

It was unnecessarily cruel, and she knew it, but it was too late. She had said it, and so far as she knew, Isis' bracelet didn't give her the ability to go back in time and stop herself from screwing up.

"You're absolutely right, Alex," Bruce said, without any apparent emotion, "You mom would have found the knife. But she's not here, and I'm all you've got now. Sorry if I'm not good enough."

Stiffly, he turned his back on her, and she knew then that she had blown it completely. The emotions boiling up inside her finally spilled over. She'd wanted to punch something before; now she let her rage get the better of her and put her fist straight through the wall.

In a Cairo hotel room, this act of vandalism would have been grounds for expulsion. In a three-and-a-half thousand year-old temple on a largely unexplored island, it was probably a mortal sin, especially if you happened to be the daughter of two esteemed archaeologists. Luckily, she was a little too old to be given up for adoption, although the expression on her father's face at that moment suggested he was seriously thinking about it.

Having heard the crunch of stone, Fusani and Rachel came rushing back in, just as Alex pulled her hand back in horror, releasing a stream of tiny stone fragments that had once represented part of ancient history.

"Whoops," she said.

"What have you done?" asked Rachel, horrified. The first words she'd said to Alex since they'd arrived on the island, and any criticisms she had to make would be completely justified, dammit.

But then she totally surprised Alex by saying, "Listen, Alex, I'm really sorry."

Wow, Alex thought. I commit an unforgivable act of vandalism, and *she's* the one that's sorry? Is this temple the entrance to Bizarro World?

"That whole thing was my fault," Rachel added.

It was the first time Alex hadn't heard a brittle, defensive tone in her voice. She wondered whether she sounded equally brittle and defensive when addressing Rachel. Probably, she realised. She realised also that this would be the perfect moment for her to apologise, too, but she just didn't feel ready. She couldn't even look at Rachel; so she kept her eyes fixed on the hole she'd just punched in the wall. The hole...

She punched it again, causing larger pieces of stone to rain down around her feet.

"Alex, stop!" Bruce yelled.

But she didn't stop. Her father's face tensed as he watched her keep on punching. Before she put on the bracelet, she would have broken every bone in her hand doing this; now it was like smashing her fist into soft cheese. Gradually, the whole wall gave way, revealing the passageway she had glimpsed behind it.

CHAPTER TWENTY-TWO

"Oh my God," said a stunned Bruce.

Fusani rushed over to Alex's side and helped pull the remaining pieces of wall away.

Alex looked to Bruce and Rachel triumphantly. Hey, she thought, if I'm lucky, maybe they'll believe the spirit if Isis told me to do that, and I wasn't just acting like a dick.

"Bruce, did you know about this?" Rachel asked.

"I had no idea. But if the knife is anywhere on this island, it's through here."

"So let's go," said Fusani, entering the passageway without fear, or maybe just without good sense. Not wishing to appear cowardly, the others joined him, though not without some trepidation.

Bruce's flashlight provided the only illumination, eventually locating a stone staircase.

"Where do you think this goes?" Alex wondered.

"It goes down," replied Fusani.

Bruce elbowed his way past the boy. Clearly, he wanted to be the first to descend, out of a sense of protectiveness and no doubt out of a desire to be the first to discover whatever the hell might be down there.

Before he and the others had taken more than a few steps down, he came to a sudden stop. Something along the wall had caught his eye. He moved the beam of light to examine it.

Alex still kept her eye on the stairs, however. She couldn't see them any longer, but she didn't trust that Set wouldn't suddenly race up them and rip her head off. It was sure dark enough for him; he'd be operating at full power in the dark. For all they knew, he probably had the Knife of Horus already-

"The Knife of Horus!" Bruce gasped. "It's here!"

OK, she thought, that simplifies matters. But then she realised that her dad was, in fact, looking at a line of hieroglyphics. He'd seen an image of the knife on the wall, she figured.

Alex and the rest of the group gathered around him. He pointed to a character she thought looked kind of like a falcon's head. So they at least knew they were heading in the right direction if they wanted to find the actual knife, something Alex already suspected and feared.

Fusani moved around Alex, pointing to something else along the wall – weird scrape-marks. Alex put her hand to the markings and realized exactly what they were - somebody's fingernails. Like someone was trying to hold onto the wall for dear life. But why?

"Dr Stone, what do you think of-"

As Fusani turned back on the step, it retracted rapidly, moving back into the staircase. Within seconds, the rest of the stairs followed suit, and the four explorers found themselves at the very top of a gigantic slide. Fusani fell backwards, and in attempting to grab him, Bruce wound up following him. The two females didn't get the chance to plan a rescue; the steps beneath them retracted, and they were heading down the chute at great speed, too. Great, thought Alex, it's the freaking Temple of Doom.

She tried to get a grip and stop her descent, but the floor was perfectly smooth – probably marble, she thought, in the seconds before she saw the chute come to a cliff-like end. She heard a massive splash as Fusani vanished over it. Her dad was about to go next, but the strap of his pack caught on a root and stopped him abruptly. As Rachel slid by, he grabbed her foot, and she skidded to a halt. Rachel, in turn, caught Alex by the arm.

"Thanks," Alex said breathlessly to her rescuer, and she really meant it. But this wasn't time for a moment; for all she knew, Fusani might be dead.

Wiping the dirt from his clothes, Bruce fumbled with his torch, eventually pointing it over the edge. Alex looked down to see that they were dangling over a large, circular underground pool. She could just about make out Fusani in the water below.

Oh crap, Alex wondered, are there piranhas in Egypt?

"Are you alright?" she called out to him. "Are you... alone?"

He motioned to them that he was okay.

"I think so," he replied. "It's too dark to see anything."

Looking around the cliff-edge, Alex noticed another passageway off to the right.

"Hold it, Dad!" she said. "Point the flashlight just there."

Bruce did as he was instructed, highlighting the depiction of another falcon head next to the entrance.

"Where the hell are we?" Rachel wondered aloud.

"Getting closer," Bruce told her. "If we can just crawl along the ledge, we can make it to that passageway."

Alex tugged at his shirt, urgently. "Dad, what about Fusani?"

"We can't help him from up here, Alex. There's got to be a way down to that pool."

He was right, she knew that. If she leapt down there to join him, she'd be just as stuck, super powers or no super powers. She could only pray to Isis that Fusani could tread water for as long as it took them to get to him.

"OK, Fusani, we're coming. Just... hold on."

As she followed her father and Rachel, she knew how weak her reassurance must have sounded, since it didn't look as though there was anything for him to hang on to. She took some small comfort from the fact that the last thing she heard before she began down the second passageway was the sound of furious paddling.

She huddled close to the others as they crept down the path, hoping all the time that they wouldn't accidentally activate any other traps – a giant boulder, or one of those poisoned darts she'd been worried about before, or whatever.

Her hopes were dashed the moment she felt something twist under her foot with the groaning noise of a stone lever finally shifting after thousands of years of inactivity. An evil-looking three-pronged spike shot out of the wall, inches above her head.

Bruce and Rachel turned in horror at the sound of her scream. Luckily for Alex, whoever planted this trap hadn't meant it for a seventeen year-old. Had she been just a few inches taller, she would have experienced an unplanned lobotomy, and she doubted Isis' bracelet would have been protection against that.

"Uh... Careful where you walk, guys," she advised the two adults.

Bruce nodded, but as soon as he took another step, Alex heard that same groaning sound that had preceded the last booby-trap. Grabbing her dad, she pulled him off his feet, just as another set of spikes came flying out in front of him.

"Good advice, Alex," he noted, breathlessly. "Everyone be careful where they walk."

He moved carefully and slowly around the protruding spikes, Rachel and Alex following on tiptoe. It seemed like an eternity before they saw the light shining from a doorway at the end of the passageway, but they had managed to avoid any unexpected piercings, and Alex was pretty sure her back wasn't covered in tarantulas. Pretty sure.

"We should be able to find Fusani from here," Bruce assured her.

He made it to the doorway unharmed, then shone the flashlight back for his female companions. As Rachel approached him, she too stepped on another trigger, leaping instantly into Bruce's arms.

"Alex, watch out!" she shouted.

More spikes flew out, barely missing Alex's face, but this time it was different – there was a skeleton impaled on this set. She screamed and jumped back in fright, triggering more spikes behind her.

"For God's sake, Alex, just stand where you are!" her father ordered.

It took about a minute for her to get her breathing under control. Or, at least, as under control as it was going to get. She was still pretty antsy, but she remembered that Fusani was counting on them. Telling herself that there was no more time to waste, she contorted her body to fit around the spikes before her. Try not to think about the skeleton, she told herself. Just imagine you're in one of those heist movies, and you're dodging red laser beams instead of... instead of... just don't think about it! I just know the tips of those things are poisoned.

***

Fusani had begun to realise that he was probably in the safest position of all the members of his party, so long as he kept swimming, and didn't swallow any of the water. If it had been there for almost four thousand years, long before the invention of chlorine.

After about fifteen minutes, he began to fear that his friends had run into some serious trouble. It may be, he considered, that their situations had become totally reversed and now *he* was going to have to rescue *them*. But if he couldn't climb out of the pool, perhaps there was another means of escape under the water. Taking the deepest breath he could manage, he sank below the surface.

***

"It doesn't make any sense," said Alex.

Light rays filtered through the cracks in the ceiling of the cavern in which, after a blessedly uneventful descent down a reassuringly stationary flight of steps, she, Bruce and Rachel found themselves. Water dripped down into a small pool off to the side. Not big enough to contain crocodiles or similar reptilian predators, Alex was relieved to note. That meant she could justify giving her full attention to the confusing object in the very centre of the room – a huge, ornate golden scale, resting on a marble platform. The scale was slightly tipped in favour of the side covered in a black substance she presumed to be dried blood. On the higher side of the scale sat a golden feather.

Alex remembered a riddle when she was a kid about a hundred tons of coal and a hundred tons of feathers, but she didn't recall anything concerning blood. Weird, but she somehow felt drawn to it.

"I don't believe it," Bruce said in amazement, "it's Osiris' Scale."

"It's beautiful," Rachel whispered.

"Who's Osiris?" she asked, running her hand along the smooth marble. It felt nice to do so when you knew you weren't sliding towards possible death.

"Osiris was the Keeper of the Dead," Rachel explained. "Upon an individual's entrance to the Afterlife, he would measure their heart. If it was lighter than a feather, they were allowed in."

Alex reasoned that there were a lot of questions regarding psychics that were probably best ignored. They hadn't played much of a part in her recent experiences, anyhow.

"So what if the heart wasn't lighter?"

"You had to spend eternity in limbo," said Bruce.

Alex raises her eyebrows. "OK... That sounds totally reasonable. And you weren't entitled to legal counsel or anything?"

Bruce waved his hand for her to be silent. He'd spotted something on the base of the scale. No, don't tell me, she thought, more glyphs.

"Here it is!" he announced. "'The Knife of Horus will be shown to those pure of heart.'"

Well, that made a certain amount of sense, Alex figured. A pretty gross kind of sense, but that was how the ancient Egyptians rolled. The only problem seemed to be that in order to find the only weapon capable of killing Set, you would have to place your heart on Osiris' Scale, and it would presumably have to be out of your body at the time, and that was never going to happen.

It was then that she noticed that her dad had taken out his pocketknife.

"You're kidding me!" she said. "You're not really going to- going to- Are you?"

"I know what I'm doing, honey," he responded.

Alex and Rachel both winced at the sight of Bruce cutting his finger open.

Tetanus shots, thought Alex, if we live through this, tetanus shots for one and all.

Carefully, he wiped his blood on the scale.

"I'm hoping this will do," he said. "It seemed to work for others."

"Bruce, are you sure this is a good idea?" Rachel sounded worried.

But Alex knew it would work. Who had a purer heart than her father? So she wasn't even a little worried when the scale began to waver. Just the gods playing mind games.

And then the side with the blood moved lower than the gold feather. Lower. That was impossible. And not fair. Totally not fair.

"Does anyone else hear that 'whooshing' sound?" Rachel asked. "It sounds kind of like wa-"

The pool exploded like a geyser, drenching them all. It obviously wasn't as shallow as Alex had imagined, since the water didn't stop coming. In fact, at this rate, it was going to fill up the cavern in just a few minutes. They'd come down here to rescue Fusani, and now they were the ones who were going to drown.

CHAPTER TWENTY-THREE

The level of the water in the cavern was still rising, but rather than lead an escape, Bruce continued to study the hieroglyphics. Alex wanted to scream at him that the meaning of the words wasn't going to change the longer he stared at it, but he wouldn't have heard her anyway. He was so wrapped up in the task, he didn't even know she was there.

"Alex, get over here."

OK, maybe he did know. Any further doubt was dispelled when he grabbed her arm and yanked her towards her. When he cut her finger with his knife, it just got creepy.

She yelped, even though, if she were being completely honest, she barely felt it. But she wanted to express her shock at his actions in some way. A drop of brilliantly red blood oozed out of the cut.

"I'm sorry about this, Alex," he told her, wiping her blood on the scale.

As before, it wavered back and forth for a moment. This time, Alex cringed. Looking round, she saw that her dad and Rachel were wearing the same pained expressions, waiting for the scale to stop. Finally, the side with the feather moved down. Bruce had been found wanting, but the Osiris' Scales decided that

Alex – chosen successor of the Goddess Isis – was pure of heart.

With relief, Bruce wiped the sweat from his forehead. The water was beginning to recede.

"Thank God," Rachel managed to say between coughs.

"Now all we have to do is rescue that damn kid," Bruce noted.

"What kid?" Fusani asked.

All three were startled to see the Egyptian teen sat on the edge of what had, until recently been the small pool; now, the water had drained off somewhere, and it had become little more than a hole in the ground.

Filled with equal measures of joy and relief, Alex threw her arms around him. She was pretty sure she hadn't broken any of his bones with her enthusiasm, but he groaned nevertheless.

"Where the hell did you spring from?" Bruce asked in amazement.

"Through there," he freed himself from Alex's grip and indicated the pool. "It's some kind of inlet from the one I fell into. I discovered it by chance, but I needed to take another gulp of air before I could explore it. I was all ready to dive again, when a massive wave appeared out of nowhere and slammed me into the wall. I was struggling to find something to hold onto – at least until I could catch my breath. I wasn't sure what had just happened, but I could only imagine it had something to do with Alex here."

Bruce shuffled his feet, awkwardly. Undoubtedly, his blood on the scale had caused the disturbance that had threatened to drown the boy.

"Then, all of a sudden, the water began to retreat. I don't know where it went to, though."

"Just be grateful the gods work for scale," Alex interjected. When no-one smiled, she wished she hadn't said anything at all.

"And that was when I saw the stone monument."

"What monument?" asked Rachel.

"It was at the very bottom of the pool, set into the floor. I thought you'd like to see it."

"It's not exactly what I was hoping for," Bruce admitted.

Alex silently agreed. She'd kind of supposed that once Osiris had run his tests on her blood, and found it to be a drop of the good stuff, the Knife of Horus would just materialize in her hands. But it didn't seem as though they were actually any closer to finding it.

"The chest was too heavy to move, but I thought that Alex-"

"*What chest?*" Rachel demanded.

"It was on top of the monument. The chest seems to be made of marble, and I couldn't even get it open..."

Bruce was more astonished than when Fusani made his sudden reappearance. "You couldn't have mentioned that part first?"

Rachel gripped Bruce's arm. To her surprise, Alex found that, under the circumstances, she was actually OK with that. "Are you thinking what I'm thinking?" she asked him.

"Only one way to find out, I guess."

"I'll be right back!" Alex announced. Without wait to hear any protestations, she leaped into the empty pool, and was soon crawling through the tunnel that led to the other pool that had nearly claimed Fusani's life earlier. She couldn't see any indications of just how the water had drained away, or where it had gone to, but at that precise moment, the crap she could give about it was probably on its way to the States at supersonic speed.

It was just as Fusani had said – even as she approached the monument, she could see carved falcon head. Oh, yeah. This must be the place, she thought with satisfaction.

The chest was of a size and shape that reminded her of an attaché case, carved out of marble – hand luggage of the Gods. Should she try to open it right now? No, her dad deserved to see this. Rachel, too. What the hell, why not? In the words of Zac Efron, *We're All in This Together*.

When she returned to the cavern with the chest, she gave her dad the opportunity to try and open it for himself, but it simply wouldn't budge.

He nodded to her. Good to know that he was sufficiently secure in his own masculinity that he could live with his daughter having ten times his strength. She pulled the lid off with ease, not even paying attention to where it fell.

All four of them crowded round the chest, marvelling at its contents.

"It's... beautiful," Alex whispered.

The hilt of the knife was pure gold, adorned with rubies and sapphires. Nobody was in the least bit surprised to see the falcon head emblazoned on it. In awe, Alex held it up. The hilt gave way to a sharp lead blade, that somehow shone, though exactly what it reflected she didn't know, since they were so far from the sunlight.

"OK... Now what?"

"Funny you should ask, sister" came the reply.

Alex didn't even have to turn around to know who had spoken. The voice had tormented her since their first encounter at the campsite. But somewhere inside, she knew it from another lifetime.

And wherever Set was, his scorpion-men must be there, too. Her dad and the others tensed. Yes, she should have known; they were so enchanted by the knife, they hadn't noticed the dark god and his two remaining foot soldiers enter.

Set swept past them to face Alex. She gave a few cautious, clumsy swipes with the blade to keep him at a distance.

"Look what I got," she said, with a smugness she definitely didn't feel. "You can't do anything now. Huh? Huh?" To the rest of her group, she hissed, "Quick, you guys, get behind me!"

"Alex, you sure you can handle this?" her dad asked. Something in his voice suggested that he didn't think she could. Recalling how close she'd come to getting her neck snapped in the Cairo sewers, she understood his doubts.

"Just do it!" she ordered, and this time they all obeyed. Rachel seemed to be taking her time, though. A gesture of defiance, Alex guessed, watching her pull off her bandanna and open her canteen, never once taking her eyes off the smirking Set. It was actually pretty cool. Weird, though... back on the bus, Rachel had said her canteen was empty.

"Be careful," Rachel warned.

"I'm on it," Alex reassured her.

"I wasn't talking to you."

The menace in her voice alerted Alex that something was way the hell up, but too late.

"What are you doing?" cried Fusani, distressed, as Rachel pressed her bandanna over Alex's mouth. It was wet with whatever had been in the canteen; not water, or Alex would have been able to fight off the attack. Instead of which she felt... like she no longer had the strength or the will to do anything. Nothing but rest, anyway. Yeah, a rest would be nice. It had been a crazy few days, and she felt like she could just sleep forever and ever.

The last thing she heard before passing out completely was Set, asking if she was alright. Or, rather, asking Isis if she was alright. But Alex was Isis, right? So that was cool.

The last thing she saw, however, was Rachel's face, rising higher and higher into the sky. Maybe it just seemed like she was going higher because Alex was falling. Yeah, that sounded right.

Funny, though, she'd never really noticed Rachel's eyes before. Those beautiful golden eyes...

CHAPTER TWENTY-FOUR

Bruce rushed to his daughter's side as she collapsed on the wet ground. Thank God, he thought, checking her; she was still breathing. With as much gentleness as was possible, he placed her head on his lap.

He glared up at Rachel, hoping to see some trace of the woman he had kissed the night before, but those golden eyes made her impossible to read. How had she hidden them? Contacts? No, he knew the answer. Magic. The power of Set.

"Traitor," spat Fusani, in a rare display of anger.

Rachel's voice was devoid of emotion, but that wasn't the only thing that struck Bruce as different about it. Her accent had changed, too. "As a high priestess of Set, I am bound to my lord," she said. "When I heard about this expedition, I knew I could somehow bring him back... But you, Bruce Stone, you did it for me."

"I trusted you," Bruce protested, feebly. She blinked. What did that blink mean? Guilt, something in her eye? Just a blink?

Like a doting parent to a gifted child, Set stroked Rachel's hair.

"You shall be remembered in the new world," he told her.

She smiled up at him.

No, Bruce realised, not like parent and child. More like master and well-behaved pet. They'd been used, then, all this time. Even after Alex stole the fragment from Set in the sewers, there was never any chance they were going to beat him to Luxor Island, not while the Dark God had Rachel on his side. Alex had been right about her, he told himself. Maybe not right for the right reasons, but right, anyway.

"It is nearly time," Set announced.

The scorpion-men seized first Fusani and then Bruce, who struggle to get out of their grip. He wouldn't leave Alex if he had the choice. Unfortunately, it looked as though he didn't. They dragged him to his feet, and Alex's head, which had been resting on his lap, slammed down onto the stone floor.

"Sorry, honey," he murmured, knowing there was no chance she could hear him.

Set lifted up her limp body, and Bruce felt loathing like he had never known before. How dare that monster touch his baby?

Set plucked the knife from Alex's hand and seemed to turn his attention to Osiris' Scale. Good luck with that, Bruce thought. I never broke a law in my life, apart from that time I sneaked into a movie theatre to watch the first *Halloween* movie, and I wasn't deemed worthy. If you go by the nickname "Dark God", what chance do you think you have?

But then Set walked straight past the scale, as though it wasn't even there. He seemed, if anything, more interested in the wall behind the scale, a wall made of seemingly normal rock. But they'd thought that when they'd first entered the temple, who knew how many feet above them. Another secret entrance made complete sense in such a senseless environment.

At Set's signal, Rachel touched one of many seemingly identical stones – how did she know which one? - and, sure enough, a portion of the wall began to move, revealing a doorway to another room.

"Chain them up out here," Set instructed his minions. "I don't need them breaking my concentration."

Bruce looked at the still-unconscious Alex. If they were to die right now, would it be better if she never woke up? Her eyelids fluttered at an alarming rate. *Wherever you are right now, honey, I hope it's a happy place.*

***

Alex couldn't remember exactly how she'd arrived back on the surface again. She recognised Luxor Island, sure, but the colours were different. Kind of muted, and they all seemed to blend into each other. *Is this what the kid in the YouTube video experienced after his dentist's appointment?*

A wind seemed to be blowing the leaves, but she couldn't seem to feel it. The plants had all given off strong fragrances when they arrived, but now she smelled nothing, nothing at all. It was like she'd wandered into a photograph. A photograph with wind blowing through it. *Right.*

No sign of the others. It took her a second to adjust to the fact that "the others" no longer included Rachel. Don't get me started on her, she thought. But there was no-one to get her started. No Dad, no Fusani. Were they dead? Was everybody dead?

If she hadn't been panicking before – and she was pretty sure she had – she definitely started to panic now. She ran. But without the wind on her face, without the feeling of the ground under her feet, there was no sensation of movement. She might just as well have been standing still, except that her surroundings altered with each step she took. This must be what it's like to be a character on the Wii, she thought. She wondered who was playing as her. Face it, who would choose me? As she reached a familiar clearing, she noticed a cloaked figure stood before the entrance to the ruins, back turned towards her. Now she knew. This is the person who would choose to play as her.

The figure turned around, and the hood fell back to reveal...

"It's you," Alex gasped.

Isis was just as she had been on her final day in the mortal realm. Her dark eyes were mesmerizing. Alex was stunned that there was actually a resemblance between them. Was that a result of the transformation, or had there always been something there? Who cares, she was face-to-face with Isis.

A faint smile appeared on the goddesses' face.

Awesome as it was, Alex didn't feel like smiling back.

"I don't know what's happened," she wailed. "I'm so lost. You have to help me!"

"No, you have to help *me*. You see, I was in your position nearly five thousand years ago, on this same island. Now you must succeed where I failed."

Tears began to well up in Alex's eyes. "Why don't you get this? I can't succeed, there's just no way! You couldn't stop Set and you're a goddess – *were* a goddess. I am so not like you. I'm just a regular person. Ordinary, you know. How am I supposed to-"

"You are far from ordinary," Isis said, firmly.

Arguing with someone so utterly magnificent didn't seem like a good idea at all, but Alex pressed on.

"Look, can I call you Isis?"

Isis didn't reply. Had Alex committed a faux pas, like farting in front of Kate Middleton? Oh well, she thought, here goes nothing.

"I'm not even supposed to be wearing your bracelet. I... kind of stole it from the tomb. This whole thing is just a huge accident."

"There are no accidents." Isis' reassurance felt to Alex like a hot shower on a cold day. "You were meant to have the bracelet. Just as you are meant to defeat my brother."

"Sounds great, and I totally get that the fate of the world depends on it, but how am I supposed to do it?"

"Set now has the Knife of Horus in his possession."

Well, isn't that just great news, Alex thought. It figured. Rachel chloroformed me, of course they could just take the knife.

"He and his high priestess led you here where he means to sacrifice you in the same manner in which he killed my father."

"High priestess, huh? Don't get me started on her. You want to know what really sticks in my craw?"

Isis didn't have to interrupt, Alex somehow knew she was about to speak, and so she should probably shut up. Just as well, since it had just occurred to her that she had no idea what a craw was.

"You must use the lead knife to stab him in the heart."

Alex nodded. "The heart, OK. And it's, uh... on the same side for gods as it is for, you know, humans, right?"

It was a grim subject to be discussing, and Alex could hardly believe she was just standing there, taking in everything Isis told her. But if she didn't do this, it'd mean the end of life on Earth – starting with her father and Fusani.

Isis smiled at her again, and it reminded her almost exactly how she felt when she'd seen her mother smile. It made her feel stronger than any superpower. Strong enough to go back, confront whatever dangers might await her beneath Luxor Island.

"You shall succeed," Isis assured her.

Something seemed to be tugging at Alex – dragging her back to the real world, back to consciousness.

Before the dream world was lost to her, she had the time to say what she'd wanted to say from the moment she encountered Isis: "You have amazing cheekbones."

And as she slid down a tunnel of smoke and darkness, she seemed to hear Isis' voice one final time.

"I know."

CHAPTER TWENTY-FIVE

The slap that brought Alex back to wakefulness made her realise that Rachel had been holding out on her. She had as much strength in her palm as those scorpion-dudes possessed in a clenched fist. Damn.

"I've been wanting to do that for quite some time now," she said, triumphantly.

Still groggy, Alex attempted to return the slap at the blur she guessed was Rachel, but found that both her arms were chained to the wall. Whatever the chains made out of, it seemed she'd finally found something she couldn't break. Double damn.

Only one thing to try – getting tough. "Let me out of these chains, High Priestess, and you can really take a crack at me. What do you say?"

As Alex's vision returned, she saw that was flanked by the two scorpion-men. Chains or not, there was no getting at her. Make that double into a triple.

As Rachel began to undo her chains, she looked to Bruce and Fusani, also chained up. Her father was barely conscious. He hadn't looked right since the scorpion sting, but it was obvious from the dark red marks all over his body that he'd received several more while she'd been away.

"What did you do to him?" she demanded, horrified.

"Not me. It was the scorpions. Set commanded it."

"Set's a dick!"

Alex wondered if she detected a hint of shame in Rachel's voice. Why did she bother insisting her father's beating wasn't her doing? Who cared? Torturing her already injured dad? She wished she had the Knife of Horus right now.

"Are you trying to kill him?" she roared. "You've got what you wanted, Rachel – you've got me! Now just let them both go!"

"When the ceremony is complete, Alex."

"And when will that be?"

"Soon enough."

Rachel returned to the hidden chamber. With the assistance of the scorpion-men, an unwilling Alex followed.

Not that either one of them would have known it, but the Temple of Set was still as beautiful as it had been almost five thousand years earlier, as though it had been held in stasis for this very moment. Alex's eyes darted about, observing the gold statues looming above them, all around. The flickering of the torches gave them the illusion of movement. At least, she hoped it was an illusion.

Atop the ornate altar, as it had been on the night Set had taken the life of his father Rah, a gold sarcophagus lay ready to receive the body of a god. And next to the altar, an urn, with a small fire beneath it. Was there something in that urn already? Lead from the mines of Anubis, maybe?

No, she assured herself. He'd been tracking them all this time. When could he have had the opportunity to get to the mines? She knew she couldn't answer that question, since she had no idea where the mines actually were. But she had to pin her hopes on something. With the scorpion-men grasping her firmly as they dragged her to the altar, there didn't seem to be anything else to count on. Well, this was just terrific; she hadn't even been conscious for five minutes, and already she'd let Isis down.

A circle of light from the sun shining through a hole in the ceiling, bathed the altar in a warm glow. Set, of course, stayed out of the light. He was now clad in an ornate black robe, grasping in his hand a golden staff in the shape of a snake. Don't they have any adorable animals on this island? Alex wondered. Of course not, they were all killed by the snakes and the scorpions.

To Alex, both the situation and the temple itself both seemed naggingly familiar. But she knew she'd never seen this place before in her life; how could she? Unless, maybe, she'd seen it in another life. It was impossible to shake the feeling that she'd somehow stepped back in time.

"Stop!" Set commanded.

His scorpion-men came to a sudden halt, though their tails continued to sway, serving as a warning to Alex of what might occur if she attempted to flee. I just need a few seconds, she thought. Break free from these goons, grab the knife from Set, slam it into his heart like Isis told me, the world is saved, and we can all go home.

Muttering an inaudible prayer, Set snapped the Knife of Horus in half and tossed both pieces into the urn.

OK, thought Alex, this represents a big problem. Too late now to start working on a Plan B. Stabbing Set with the knife was pretty much Plans A thru Z. *Now* what do I do? At least I won't have to apologise to Isis – if I go anywhere after death, I doubt it's to where the gods and goddesses hang out.

As the knife began slowly to melt in the urn, the beam of light that shone in upon them grew ever smaller. A shadow was beginning to cover the sun. Alex frowned. Was there an eclipse scheduled for today? An eclipse meant total blackness... and that meant Set would be stronger than ever. Now, she realised, there was truly no hope for her, for any of them.

"No!" she screamed. Given the circumstances, she could no longer think of anything else to do.

Without warning, Rachel punched her in the stomach, knocking the wind out of her. The slap, she realised, had been nothing. The punch really hurt. Really.

Set seemed not to have noticed. His attention was focussed elsewhere. "Isn't the eclipse *painfully* beautiful?" he asked no-one in particular.

Gliding over to Alex, he caressed her face. Alex found it hard to imagine a more revolting sensation. She actually preferred it when he'd been punching her. She shuddered in disgust at his attentions.

"Soon you shall no longer bear this heavy burden, sister."

Alex lacked the strength to point out to Set that she wasn't his sister, and if she'd even suspected there was the remotest chance of it, she'd have demanded a blood test.

Releasing her, he turned away, heading back up to the altar.

"Bring her to me," he ordered.

Alex made one last attempt to struggle with her scorpion-captors, but it was no good, she was just too weak. Whatever Rachel got me with, she considered, it wasn't just chloroform. Not that she'd ever been chloroformed before, but her new body seemed impervious to pretty much everything else, it seemed unlikely she could be taken down by something so simple. Such issues really didn't matter anymore, though. She was dragged in front of Set and forced to her knees, not that it took a lot of force to do that.

He could kill her right now, she knew. Why the hell had he snapped the Knife of Horus in two, then? Why had he tossed it into the urn to melt? Because he wanted to do something else with it – something that required molten lead.

Before she could try to think what that could be, Set grabbed her below her shoulders and, as he had done in the Cairo sewers, raised her into the air. At least he wasn't picking her up by the hair this time, so it was more annoying than it was painful. She kicked him repeatedly, but if he even felt it, he gave no indication. His grip was like a vice. She'd been nauseous enough before, but seeing the temple from this weird angle, there was a very real danger she might throw up. And unless she could do that over Set himself, that would be pretty undignified and pointless.

Looking down at him, she could see that he was muttering another prayer under his breath. Before she had the chance to ask herself exactly who a god prays to, he dropped her into the sarcophagus, chuckling with malicious glee. Free from his grip, Alex knew that this was her one and only chance to escape and thwart Set's plans. But those plans proved to be pretty damn unthwartable. Chains, no doubt made of the same substance that held her captive earlier, were locked around her arms and legs before she had a chance to do anything.

Checking the progress of the urn, Set blew on the small fire beneath it. The flames quickly intensified. It wouldn't be long before the knife had melted completely – perfect for his purposes. There was no chance of help arriving, particularly since the only person in the world capable of defying him would shortly dissolve completely once the molten lead from the mines of Anubis was poured over her heart.

***

Bruce banged his head against the wall repeatedly, hoping that the pain in his skull would distract him from the pain he was feeling throughout his body, the result of repeated stinging. Of course, the problem was, the more his head ached, the more he found it harder to think. In the unlikely event that there was a way out of this situation, it would never come to him in time. And Alex needed him. Oh, Alex...

"Dr Stone, are you alright?"

Bruce lacked the strength to give Fusani's query the disdain it deserved. Instead, he simply shook his head, which hurt as much as he expected.

He attempted to say, "We have to help her," but what came out was little more than an incoherent noise and a few drops of bloody saliva. He used what little energy he had left to rattle his chains.

Fusani imitated his actions. There was no give in the chain itself, but Bruce couldn't help noticing that the link fastening the chain to the wall was slightly loose. He wanted to tell the kid as much, but the most he could manage was a grunt. But it was enough; Fusani noticed it, too. He wrapped as much of the chain as he could around his left arm, and began tugging furiously at the link.

"That's it," Bruce finally managed to say. "Keep going, Fusani. I've got an idea."

***

Inside the sarcophagus, Alex was engaged in a similarly futile battle with the bonds that held her immobile. I snapped that security guard's cuffs without blinking, she thought, so what gives? Nothing gives, that's the problem.

Eyeing the eclipse, she noticed a sliver of the sun shining down just below her ankle. A possibility occurred to her. Set's power came from darkness, didn't they? Maybe they did, maybe they didn't, but he sure was a whole lot stronger in the dark. Was the same true of his cuffs? Was that why not even the power of Isis could shatter them? She honestly had no idea, but it was the only thing she could do. Feeling almost as foolish as she was terrified, Alex began to wriggle, trying to slide her cuffed ankle into the light.

When Set's incomprehensible prayers came to a sudden stop, she figured she was busted. She froze, but was surprised to find that she could still hear the sound of someone struggling against metallic shackles. Dad and Fusani, she realised. They were still outside, attempting to get free. Hopefully, doing a better job than I am, she thought, though she thought it unlikely.

"I can't work under these conditions," Set complained. "The mortal needs another dose."

She freaked out on hearing this. No way could her dad survive another scorpion sting, no way. She tried with all her might to break the cuffs, pictured herself leaping out of the sarcophagus, racing to Bruce's aid. No good. She was trapped.

There was only one thing left to do, and that was plead. Not with Set, though, he obviously had no concept of pity. But maybe someone else...

"Rachel," she yelled. "Rachel, can you hear me? Please, Rachel, you can't do it. He'll die. You know he'll die!"

There was silence. Had Alex got through to her? She wished she could lift her head up far enough to see what was going on. Then, she heard Rachel say, "You!" Presumably, she was addressing a scorpion-man. "Follow me."

Alex felt like screaming in exasperation. How many times would she fail before the world came to an end?

CHAPTER TWENTY-SIX

Bruce was groaning, his eyes rolled up in his head, as Rachel and the scorpion-man approached. Whatever he'd been planning, it was plain he'd exhausted himself in the attempt.

Rachel nodded to her half-human companion, whose tail rose, shuddering, in preparation for the final sting.

But it was suddenly in no position to deliver the fatal dose of venom. Fusani threw his chain around both its tail and neck, and did his best to strangle the beast before Rachel could stop him.

Struggling to free itself, the scorpion-man succeeded only in pulling Fusani's chains from the wall, enabling him to tighten his grip until there was no longer anyone to fight with, just a large pile of dust at his feet.

Rachel would have leapt at the boy, but Bruce summoned up the strength to trip her. As she fell to the ground, he grabbed her, pulling her into him. There was no way he could fight her, of course, he knew that; he just had to be at the right angle to avoid her elbows, which, if aimed correctly, could probably drive a hole through his gut.

"Bruce, let me go!" she demanded, furiously.

He couldn't help but smile at her annoyance. Yes, sir, he thought, I may be about forty per-cent scorpion toxin, but I'm still in the game. He ripped the keys from her belt.

"You don't actually believe Set's going to take care of you once he gets his powers, do you?" he asked as they struggled. "You weren't this naïve before you got your golden contacts, Rachel. You've got to be kidding me. You're just a pawn, expendable, totally useless!"

It was an insult too far. "That's... enough!" she roared, twisting round to grab Bruce's head, and slam it hard into the wall. He was in so much pain already that the impact barely registered with him. Things must really be bad, he thought, if I'm viewing that as a plus.

He watched her rush back into the Temple of Set, realising that she could just as easily have snapped his neck. If his full faculties ever returned, he'd devote some time to wondering why she hadn't.

***

"Master, forgive me."

Alex still couldn't see what was happening, but Rachel sounded pretty frazzled, which could only mean that her boys were still alive and still fighting. Awesome.

"No more," Set ordered her. "I already know what happened. I wasted one of my minions for you." Alex grinned at this news. Yay, team.

"Sometimes I think I only brought you here because the scorpion-men are unable to speak," Set told Rachel. "And now I don't want to listen to you."

"Master, I implore you. What can I do to be in your graces once again?"

Alex didn't know or care what Rachel could do (although she knew what she'd like her to do, which involved an infeasible amount of Semtex stuffed into an unlikely orifice), but she took advantage of this distraction to throw her whole body towards the light. Her father and Fusani had given her the time to take this one final chance, and she wasn't going to waste it.

She heard Set say, "You have done enough." She just hoped these industrial relations problems would keep him distracted a little while longer.

A choking noise alerted her to the seriousness of Rachel's plight. Alex gulped, remembering the strength Set possessed. Now there was someone else who needed rescuing. Not long now, Alex thought. Almost in the light... Almost...

"I thought you would remember me... in the new world?" Rachel's voice was barely recognisable under the pressure Set was exerting.

At last, the sun's rays caught Alex's ankle!

"Indeed, I *shall* remember you," Set assured Rachel, calmly.

As Alex fidgeted with the cuff, she heard the sickening crunch of bone, followed by Rachel's lifeless body dropping to the floor.

The cuff finally weakened enough for Alex to free her left leg. How much longer would she have until Set turned his attentions back onto her, she wondered. She could hear no sign of him, which she found extremely worrying. I can't stop now, she thought, beginning to work on her right leg.

***

Bruce was unlocking the chains around Fusani's wrists when he spotted Set in the doorway. He and the boy immediately stood back against the wall, bracing themselves against whatever that black-hearted son-of-a-bitch might throw at them.

"Where's Alex?" Fusani asked, fearlessly.

Set smiled at the boy.

"You should both know, I admire your perseverance, and your intelligence. It's almost as though you expect to live forever. But that is not within the scope of mere mortals. Permit me to demonstrate."

Here it comes, thought Bruce, knowing there was no way to adequately prepare oneself for becoming nothing more than a bloody smear on a wall.

But Set's actions were less dramatic than he anticipated. The Dark God turned his attention to Osiris' Scale, which had earlier seemed of no interest to him. Dropping his snake-like staff, Set produced a small, short-bladed knife from beneath his cloak. Both Bruce and Fusani held their breath, as Set sliced his own hand. Blood began trickling onto the scale.

Fascinating, Bruce thought. He'd already predicted what would happen, and if gods can drown like us mere mortals... Well, I'm willing to pay that price for Alex's sake. Just a pity about Fusani. In a few seconds, it'll start. The water will fill the room again, and I can get to watch that bastard's lungs fill with water.

Before the process began, though, Set strode back into the Temple. The moment Bruce saw what was happening, he limped after Set, arriving too late to stop the stone door closing firmly, locking them in.

"Dammit!"

Fusani joined him, both attempting to find the stone that opened the door, but it was no good. It obviously wasn't just a question of simply pushing the right one, like something out of a gothic romance, it was clearly more complex. Why hadn't he paid more attention when Rachel was doing it?

"Uh, Dr Stone..."

Fusani directed his attention to the scale. Just as before, when Bruce had placed his own blood on it, it teetered. There was no chance of Set being found worthy, not unless the gods operated a severely messed-up system. What was he thinking? That was the only way they'd survive.

The side of the scale containing Set's blood slammed all the way down, leaving the gold feather side dangling in the air.

Then came the familiar rush of water. If anything, it seemed faster this time. It had reached the level of their ankles in seconds – the scales had recognised a true sinner.

"Didn't Set leave his staff behind?" asked Fusani.

"Yes!"

"I can't believe he forgot it."

It was impossible to be certain, with the noise the water was making, but Bruce imagined he could hear the hissing of a snake, somewhere in the chamber with them.

"You know, Fusani, I'm not sure he did forget it."

The water now splashed around their knees.

CHAPTER TWENTY-SEVEN

Set peered into the urn. Most of the Knife of Horus had turned to boiling lead, but there was still about three inches of blade remaining. When he had murdered his own father, he'd had longer to prepare than this. And while it was true that he'd been planning this act for several thousand years, he'd lacked the physical form necessary to take care of the small details. But his sister had to be dispatched once and for all before the eclipse ended. There really was no more time to waste.

Even touching the urn would have given any ordinary person severe burns, but Set carried it over to the sarcophagus without even minor discomfort.

No more time to waste, he had told himself, but what kind of brother would he be if he didn't take just a final moment to acknowledge his sister's impending destruction? Leaning over the sarcophagus, he saw Alex, still shackled, of course.

"Give Rah my regards, Isis," he whispered.

Not even any armour to remove before the lead could be poured. In choosing the form of this wretched girl to house her essence, her sister had made it far too easy. But, then, hadn't he waited so long for this? Wasn't it only fair that the final stage should be easy? He began to tip the urn.

Alex kicked it out of his hands before even a drop of lead could spill on her. Terrified of what it might do to him, Set stumbled backwards, landing on top of his remaining scorpion-servant, which promptly evaporated, the impact having killed it instantly.

The moon had moved further off the sun, revealing more light. Now completely free of the influence of Rachel's drug, Alex used the extra surge of strength to free her arms. As she launched herself from the sarcophagus, she was ready to fight. Set swatted her from the air like an irritating insect.

Wow, that didn't work too well, Alex thought, backing up as he rounded on her. Good thing no-one's watching this: they might get the impression I was getting my butt kicked.

"You always have to make things difficult, don't you?"

"Yeah, that's what my dad says, too."

Another firm slap sent her sliding across the temple.

"I killed *my* father."

"Maybe if he'd hugged you, you wouldn't have grown up to be such a tool," she suggested, clambering up the wall. She'd recovered her strength, but her ability to feel pain seemed more acute also. I had the advantage for, like, half a second back there, she told herself. What the hell did I do wrong?

She looked round the temple, trying to find some weapon she could use against Set. Her glance passed over Rachel's dead body - she reminded herself to have some feelings about that at some point, if she survived. Eventually, she focussed upon the urn, which lay on its side by the altar. There was the Knife of Horus – or, anyway, half of the Knife of Horus. OK, not even half. Let's just say *some* of the knife. Maybe it would be enough.

Set took another swipe at her, but this time she was prepared. Rather than stand and fight, though, she avoided his fist, and made for the knife. Set struck the wall behind her, sending a crack running up through the rock.

***

By the time the water had reached the level of their waists, Bruce and Fusani had tried all the stones that might open the door to Set's Temple. With no other options, and no way of knowing what Set might be doing to Alex, they began to check again, more frantically than before, if possible.

There's got to be a special technique, Bruce thought. Please don't say it's palm-print activated, or DNA-encoded, or some crap like that.

It was as he was panicking thus that a live asp that had once been Set's wooden staff brushed his leg as it swam past.

He gasped.

"What is it?" Fusani asked.

"I just felt something touch my leg!"

"Maybe it was the staff Set dropped."

"Yeah, maybe."

Bruce turned back to the wall again. The boy's right, he told himself, it was probably just the staff.

Or the scorpion-man. No, it faded away into dust. The staff, then. He tried to ignore the fact that what touched him it hadn't felt like an inanimate object; it felt alive.

The snake collided with Fusani, pushing him into the wall. "That was something living!"

Bruce nodded. "I was afraid of that. Just keep calm, kid, I'm trying to get us out of here."

"I'm serious, Dr Stone, there is something in the water!"

The asp broke the surface of the water, flicking its tongue hungrily. Screaming, the two bolted away from the door as it struck, striking its head against the rock.

Bruce hoped that the damn thing might have knocked itself out, or at least be slightly stunned by the collision. But, of course, it wasn't technically a living creature at all, and he had no way of knowing whether it could feel pain. But he didn't doubt its ability to cause pain. The asp ducked under the water, with no indication of where it might be headed.

He and Fusani look around the cavern, wildly searching the water, but it was impossible to see beneath the surface. The water was now up to their chests. In a couple more minutes, Bruce considered, it wouldn't matter whether they'd evaded the asp; they'd be just as dead.

"Where is it? Where'd it go?" For the first time since he'd met the boy, Fusani seemed genuinely panicked. He was holding a pocketknife in his hand, making futile stabbing motions at nothing whatever.

"I don't know where it went, but right now, we have to find a way out of here before we drown! Back to the door!"

Bruce didn't even notice the snake heading for him as he once again resumed his seemingly hopeless task. He lost about five years from his life when Fusani attempted to alert him by tapping him on the shoulder. "Christ, kid! I thought you were the snake!"

"I just saw it again! It's over th-"

But once again, the asp had gone.

I'm sick of this, Bruce thought, twisting his fist against the wall in frustration, sick of these games. Wait, was that the sound of the door mechanism? Had he found the right rock, touched it in just the right way?

"Fusani! I think I did it!" He began to laugh. "I think we're going to be alright!"

Fusani had only a second to take in this news before he was pulled underwater, the pocketknife flying from his hand as he submerged.

CHAPTER TWENTY-EIGHT

Fight analysts are free to debate the question of whether gallons of water spilling into the Temple of Set - along with two males and a vicious asp - might have altered the balance of the battle between Alex and Set in favour of one or the other; all Alex knew was that she was delighted and relieved to have her father and her best friend back.

Set took advantage of this bizarre incident to slam her against the wall. She clawed at him wildly, managing to somehow free herself, but also ripping open his robe in the process. She was too busy fighting for her life to wonder where the huge snake that was now heading for her dad and Fusani had come from, but she was able to yell, "Dad, behind you!" before Set's fist struck her jaw.

Upon hearing Alex's warning, Bruce spun round, and was greeted by the asp's gaping jaws, but he didn't allow the sight to freeze him to the spot; instead, he kicked the serpent full in the mouth.

Go, Chuck Norris, thought Alex with pride, dodging several more punches from her adversary. As the asp recoiled from Bruce's kick, Fusani scrabbled around for his pocketknife. The snake sprang at Bruce again, but the boy leapt, stabbing it under the neck, and twisting the blade until both the snake and Fusani fell on top of Bruce, who barely had enough strength to say, "Ouch."

Alex was too distracted by all this to notice that Set was hidden in one of the darker corners, and had now achieved the strength necessary to push over one of the large golden statues that lined the temple.

Exhausted from his tussle with the asp, Fusani looked up just in time to see that the statue was falling towards Alex. "Watch out!" he cried.

Without even turning to see what threatened her, Alex rolled out of the way. The statue came crashing down on the exact spot she had been standing, moments earlier.

"You missed me," Alex announced, as Set's foot connected with the back of her head, sending her tumbling to the ground.

"You will never defeat me, sister," Set noted, superciliously, "I'm simply too strong for you."

She was just inches from the urn now. And beyond that was what remained of the knife. She strained to reach it, but Set saw what she was trying to do, and stopped her by slamming her head against the ground with such violence it would have crushed the skull of an ordinary person.

Bruce and Fusani cried out for him to stop, but both were too weak to do anything about it. Alex knew that, despite the ringing in her ears, she was the only one left who could do anything about it. Just her. World ain't gonna save itself, she thought. If

I can't reach the knife, I just have to work with what I've got.

Grabbing the urn, she put all the force she possessed behind swinging it at Set's head. The sound of the collision was not unlike the tolling of a massive bell. And from the howl he emitted, she knew she'd given as good as she'd gotten.

"Payback, jerk!"

She dropped the urn, which now had a considerable dent in it, in favour of the Knife of Horus, its blade now a mere inch in length. It had better be enough, she told herself.

Set, it seemed, was not simply boasting when he told Alex he was the stronger. It seemed he was already recovering from the attack. Grabbing the side of the sarcophagus, he began to pull himself up. Alex knew it was now or never.

"Let me give you a hand, brother!"

Grabbing his legs, she tipped him into the sarcophagus before he knew what was happening. She daren't hesitate now. Everything depended upon striking now, and striking hard. She raised the knife above her head.

"This is for Isi-"

Set's arm shot up and grabbed her throat. He wasn't going to give in now; he was going to do to her what he'd done to Rachel. She felt his fingers press hard against her larynx. Don't struggle, Alex, just do what you have to do! Was that *her* voice? Who cares? Do it now!

She saw Set's eyes widen in fear as she rammed the blade into his chest, forcing it in all the way to the hilt. With a massive spasm, he threw Alex off. She landed hard on the ground, fearing that the knife hadn't been long enough to do its job. But then she saw that she was showered with dust. Dust that had once been Set's outstretched arm.

"That's nasty."

Cautiously, she peered over the edge of the sarcophagus to see Set lifeless and gradually disintegrating, a stunned expression on what was left of his face.

"Yeah. Nasty."

The eclipse was over. Daylight poured in through the hole in the ceiling, directly onto the corpse of the Dark God. Alex refused to take her eyes off the remains of Set's remains, so she didn't see what became of Rachel, but when she finally plucked up the courage to look away, she saw her father running his finger through a patch of dust on the floor of the temple.

A clank of metal from the sarcophagus made her spin round. Typical, she thought; the bad guy always comes back at the last possible second. But he hadn't; the hilt of the Knife of Horus had fallen all the way through Set's crumbling body. There was nothing else left, not even the bracelet Set had stolen from his father, Rah.

I guess that qualifies as dead, thought Alex.

"So, guys," she said to the others, "we just saved the world. What else do you wanna do today?"

"Honestly?" Bruce replied. "I think I'd like to go to hospital. We can't all be superheroes, you know."

She was suddenly aware that her arm was tingling, growing ever warmer. Looking down, she realised it wasn't actually her arm – it was Isis' bracelet. She gasped with pain as it became unbearably hot. Was this some last "screw-you" of Set's? Would she end up a pile of dust, too?

Then, as the heat faded away, so did the bracelet itself. Soon, all that remained was a hieroglyphic tattoo. It glowed silver for a moment before fading to black.

"Awesome," she whispered. Her father had forbidden her from getting any tats – he'd been pretty annoyed when he mistook a squashed spider for one - but she couldn't see how he could object to this. She didn't actually feel any different for the loss of the bracelet, and a quick glance told her that she still had her incredible bod, but was that it? Was she no longer special?

"Alex, are you alright?" Bruce asked, placing his hands on her shoulders. It was comforting, especially after she'd spent most of the last couple of days getting the holy snot kicked out of her.

She nodded, aware that tears were welling up in her eyes. He pulled her into a full embrace.

"I'm so sorry. God, I'm so sorry, Alex."

She stayed in her father's arms for about a minute. She wished it could be all day, but Luxor Island wasn't exactly the best place to get him medical attention. With regret, she pulled away from him, and wiped her eyes. She was comforted to see that he did the same.

"I think Cleopatra has a rival," said Fusani, stepping in to get a hug from Alex, too. She was happy to oblige. She was equally happy to oblige when he leaned in even closer. She felt an entirely different sort of tingle. It's finally going to happen, she told herself. My first kiss, on a deserted island, in the temple of an Egyptian god. She closed her eyes, and willed it to come.

When it didn't, she opened them again, to find that her dad had yanked Fusani back by the ear.

"Oh, I don't think so, lover boy" he said.

Alex didn't complain; she just laughed. She was sure there'd be another time.

Reaching inside the sarcophagus, Bruce picked up the hilt, and inspected it. "One last artefact," he observed.

"What do you say we take it to go?" Alex suggested. A pebble bounced off her forehead. "What the-?"

More stones began to fall, larger ones. The Temple was crumbling around them.

"Oh, you've got to be kidding me!" she complained. "This is so bogus!"

Fusani grabbed her hand, as they ran for the exit.

CHAPTER TWENTY-NINE

The roof was getting lower and lower as they raced through the maze of tunnels, Alex supporting her wounded father. She and Fusani were so busy trying to anticipate where the rocks that fell at an increasing rate might land, that they almost didn't stop in time. A rumbling from below was all the warning they had before a huge gap opened up in the path before them.

"You go first!" Bruce insisted.

Alex knew that if her dad wasn't the first across, the gap would only widen, and he wouldn't be able to jump at all. Without waiting for further debate, she grabbed him by the collar and hurled him across to the other side.

Wow, she thought. Was that a super-powered throw, or just love and adrenaline? Figure it out on the surface, just focus on getting the hell out of here.

"What are you waiting for?" Bruce asked. "Jump!"

Fusani motioned for her to go next. More rocks tumbled down. Well, she was sure he was capable of making the leap, so why shouldn't she jump first?

She cleared the gap without difficulty, landing in her dad's arms.

"Miss me?" she asked with a grin.

Fusani didn't waste a second in following her. As his feet touched the edge, it gave way beneath him. Alex shrieked, as she saw him begin to tumble backwards, his arms flailing wildly. She grabbed him by his belt, and yanked him back onto semi-solid ground.

She wished she could have thrown her arms around him right then and sobbed with relief, but there was no time to spend on emotional outpourings. In fact, now that she knew exactly what she wanted to say to the men in her life, there didn't seem to be time to do anything but run. And the cave-in was still coming their way.

"I think I see daylight!" Bruce cried. "Almost there, guys! Come on!"

***

They watched from what they hoped was the nearest safe spot on the island as the ruins sank rapidly into the earth, leaving behind just a large pile of rocks. Ruins of ruins.

Too bad Dad threw away his phone, Alex thought. That meant no pictures. We're the only three living people who ever saw that place. And by "living", I mean just barely. She flopped back on the ground with an enormous sigh of relief.

"What a day."

But even then, they couldn't stop to rest for long. The captain of the *Nefertiti* had said he'd be back for them before sunset. None of them seemed confident that he was telling the truth, but, really, what choice did they have? It was either that, or they stuck around and wound up as relics themselves.

It was as they were trudging through the foliage - Alex leading, Fusani helping Bruce - that they heard the faint sound of an idling motor.

Alex looked back at the guys, and saw their faces light up.

"Do you think it's him?" she asked, and then felt foolish. Who else could it be?

With renewed strength, she ran ahead of them, and burst into the clearing to see the *Nefertiti* – now officially the most beautiful vessel ever constructed - anchored in the shallow waters.

The aged captain waved from at her from the hull. Alex waved back, then looked over her shoulder as an overjoyed Bruce and Fusani emerged.

Together, they waded through the water to the ship, laughing like imbeciles. The captain threw down a ladder for them.

"Sunset's not for a few more hours," Bruce pointed out to him.

"True," he replied, "But I thought that if I waited till then, I wouldn't have any passengers. This island'll eat you alive."

"It tried," said Alex, grabbing hold of the ladder.

***

"So... did you find what you were looking for?"

Bruce, lying exhausted, on the deck, shared a smile with his daughter. "Yes. Yes, we did."

Oblivious of any sentiment in his passenger's tone, the captain simply said, "Alright then, let's turn her around."

He left for the control room.

Alex took one last look at Luxor Island, knowing that it would never again form part of her vacation plans.

"You ready to go home, yet, honey?" her father asked her.

She nodded. "A trip to Aunt Carol's is looking pretty good to me right now."

He laughed and put his arm around her. She'd pictured this kind of family bonding moment back at Northwood, never imagining that they'd have to go to hell and back to achieve it.

"When we get back, what do you say we go explore that hiking trail that's supposed to be great this time of year?" Bruce suggested.

"Sounds good, Dad. But can we spend a few days just watching TV first? I've got practically a whole season of *Glee* on TiVo."

"*Glee*... Is that the one that's kind of like *Fame*?"

"I don't know. What's *Fame*?"

He groaned. "God, I feel old. Look, honey, we can do whatever you want. I just want you to know I'm going to be around a lot more from now on."

She rested her head on his shoulder. He moaned with pain, but wouldn't let her move it.

Glancing down at the hieroglyphic tattoo on her wrist, he asked, "Any chance that thing can be lasered off?"

"Probably not. I think it's, you know, magic. Besides, it's my only souvenir of our trip to Egypt."

Bruce rummaged in his pocket and produced the hilt. "Not the only souvenir."

CHAPTER THIRTY

Alex's mind was elsewhere as her father's black Mercedes SUV screeched to a halt in the Northwood School parking lot. There was a lot she could be thinking about, but it was the farewell at Cairo Airport that stayed with her, even after all this time. It was where it had all begun for her, and it was where she'd expected- Well, did it really matter? Obviously, it did, or she wouldn't still be thinking about it.

***

Bruce had shared a tight handshake and a warm smile with Fusani. After what seemed like months wearing the same sweat-stained filthy clothes (more like rags than clothes at the very end of their adventure), the simple act of showering and changing clothes seemed to each of them like the greatest thing in the world. Second greatest, after medicine and bandages, of course.

Bruce had undergone an extensive course of anti-venom, and Fusani's arm had been put in a sling. Alex had been checked and pronounced fit. Even by the standards of a superhero – which she guessed she maybe still was – she felt like crap, but her injuries were healing without much treatment.

"It's been a pleasure meeting you, Fusani," said Bruce, as though they'd finished a business negotiation instead foiling the plans of an evil Egyptian god. "I've enjoyed your company."

"Likewise, Dr Stone," he replied.

When her father released his hand and stepped back, Alex moved in, teary-eyed and determined not to be so formal in her goodbye. She hugged Fusani warmly.

"You promise to write to me?"

"I don't have e-mail," he replied, a smirk in his voice.

She hit him playfully, making sure to strike his good arm. "Seriously, you're coming to visit, right?"

"Then you can be *my* tour guide, Alex. Somewhere exciting for a change, please."

She blinked away her tears and smiled back at him. She'd miss that smile most of all. When things seemed at their worst, it was the one thing she could rely on. As he leaned forwards, she knew she wasn't going to close her eyes this time. When the kiss came, she would be ready.

Fusani came to a sudden stop before their lips met. He was no longer looking at her, but something behind her. What? Alex looked over her shoulder to see her dad giving the boy a stern look. Seriously?

With Bruce's approval, Fusani returned Alex's hug, adding a brotherly pat on her back, which only furthered her annoyance. The hell with this, she thought. When he tried to disengage, she refused to let him go. She heard the sound of her dad clearing his throat, but she decided to ignore it. If there was no kiss coming her way, she was at least going to enjoy as much contact as she could get.

"Um... Alex, honey? We need to go. We don't want them taking off without us."

As if conspiring with him, the tannoy announced it was indeed time for them to board the plane. With regret, she slowly released Fusani, and felt like crying all over again.

"I'll see you soon, Alex," he assured her. Nodding, she'd followed her dad through the terminal, frequently looking back to see Fusani waving. It was too far away to see whether he was still smiling, but she knew instinctively that he was.

That was my moment, she knew with sadness, that was my moment and I walked away from it.

***

"I'll be here at three-thirty, honey. On time, I promise. Hey, you still with us?"

Her thoughts returning to the present, Alex gave Bruce a smile and a quick hug – not like the hug she'd shared with Fusani at the airport, but still good.

"Okay, now run, or you'll be late!"

That, at least, hasn't changed, she thought, grabbing her books and leaping out of the car.

People stopped and stared at her as she ran through the quad, but this time nobody was laughing at the awkward girl with the frizzy hair. Once again, she grinned at how much she probably looked like a shampoo ad, her glossy hair blowing back in the wind. Wish I was in slow-motion, how awesome would that be?

"Hey, did Frizzball get a makeover?"

Even as she passed by them without looking, Alex recognized Ellen's voice, and sarcastic tone.

"I think she straightened her hair or something," her partner-in-crime Nikki suggested. "You're still, like, ten times prettier. She tries too hard."

Actually, Nikki, I wouldn't want to try to impress you at all, Alex thought to herself. If there was ever a time when I cared what you think – or even *if* you think – then it's over now.

With the thump of Ellen's foot connecting angrily with a soccer ball, life really did go into slow-motion for Alex. Onlookers shared a joint gasp as they watched the ball sail through the air, about to collide with the back of her head. Their reaction when she spun round and head-butted it right back, nailing Ellen in the head and sending her sprawling, was a mixture of cheers and laughter.

Alex thought at first that the running feet pursuing her belonged to Ellen, furious at having been robbed of what passed for dignity, but no - she could still hear Ellen crying out, "Somebody do something!"

No, it was Nikki who had caught up with her

"Hey, Alex, wait up! I think we have first period together. Want to walk with me?"

Not wanting to get into a conversation with her, Alex walked through the door, allowing it to slam in Nikki's face.

***

"So we're not banished to the back this year?" asked Shannon. She was sat next to Alex on the second row, and had already expressed concern that she might start feeling light-headed.

"I thought I'd change it up a bit," Alex explained.

"I like it. You look good, Alex. What am I saying, you look gorgeous. I think maybe I need to spend the summer in Egypt, too. And you got a tat, you, little rebel! Can't believe Indiana Jones allowed it."

"Dad didn't really have a say. There's kind of a story behind it."

"I'll bet. Well, I like it. It's exotic. You noticed Chris is looking good, too, right?"

Actually, she hadn't. She noticed him now, as he entered the class with Nikki. Yes, he was looking good – even a little more toned than before, if that was possible – but nothing he had could compare with the smile of a seventeen year-old Egyptian she couldn't seem to stop thinking about.

"Is this seat taken?" asked Chris, all poised to sit next to Alex. This time, she was sure his decision wasn't based on a lack of availability; all of a sudden, she was more to him than just a girl who looked as though she might have a pen.

She shrugged. "It's all yours. Help yourself."

"Alex, right?" he asked as he sat.

"Uh-huh."

Shannon's eyes were bulging. She seemed more excited than Alex. Then again, maybe they were bulging with astonishment that Alex wasn't more excited. And it was true, Alex knew. Not so long ago, she had entertained a fantasy about Chris. Now, she struggled to recall it.

"I just love your highlights," offered Nikki, seated behind her, having apparently forgotten the door-to-the-face incident mere minutes earlier. "Who's your stylist?"

"I don't have highlights," Alex replied, without turning round.

"Wow, then you are so lucky. I mean, it took me six months to get my hair to look like this, and even I still sometimes have to get lowlights..."

Alex let her witter on this vein, neither knowing nor caring whether Nikki realised she was no longer listening. She imagined that no-one really listened to Nikki. It was rude, yes, but the truth was that Nikki had never wanted to talk to her before today. Now Alex knew for definite that it was just as well, since she had absolutely nothing to say.

Thankfully, Mr Willowby entered as the bell rang, and Nikki was, with some prompting, obliged to put an end to her noise pollution.

"Back to the grind," the teacher grumbled to himself, setting down his briefcase. "Alright, class, before we delve into European history..."

Most of the class groaned. Shannon clapped her hands in excitement.

"... let's hear how your summer vacation went."

Nikki's hand shot up into the air. The temptation to speak, and, more importantly, to speak about herself, was just too strong.

"Nikki, you're up."

"Well, as you all remember I vaycayed with Ellen in the Hamptons, where we had mad parties and got super tan."

Alex didn't remember that at all. She'd just remembered never having heard the word "vaycay" before.

"Anybody else?" asked Willowby.

"I travelled through Switzerland and France," Shannon volunteered.

"Well that's great, Shannon. I bet you'll be a big help this semester."

At the sound of a moan, the whole class turned as one to witness Ellen walking in, a bag of ice clamped to her head, courtesy of the school nurse. Seeing Chris sat next to Alex, she said nothing, but shambled off to the back of the room.

"Alex, why don't you tell us about your summer?" asked Willowby. "I understand it was pretty exciting." From his briefcase he produced a copy of *National Geographic* with Alex and her father on the cover. Not that anyone in the class save for Shannon cared to read it, but the caption beneath the picture read "Dr Stone and Daughter Discover Egyptian Tomb; Their Harrowing Journey into Ancient Mythology."

"I helped my dad excavate a tomb, took a trip down the Nile, saved the world. You know, just stuff."

"I understand that, thanks to you, Luxor Island has now become a tourist resort."

"Yeah, but only on the southern side, and it's not a good idea to stay too long," she told him. "Also, they rip you off big-time at the gift shop."

***

It had been a good day, probably the first really good one Alex had had at Northwood, if you didn't count the time that Chris set off the fire alarm on a dare, and pupils and faculty had to spend most of the afternoon outside in the sunshine.

Shannon had pressed her for details of her Egyptian adventure, and who could blame her? If their positions had been reversed, Alex would have been equally full of questions. But there was no way she could give a decent account of everything that had happened to between lessons. So she'd promised instead that they would have a long talk about it that night. As they hugged goodbye, Shannon reminded her to call, and to hold nothing back. Nothing at all? That covers a lot of ground, she thought.

Looking out over the parking lot, she was glad to spot a familiar black Mercedes SUV waiting for her. She never doubted him for a second, she told herself, putting away her cell phone.

As she started down the steps, she heard Chris call out, "Alex, wait up!"

He was running after her. She honestly never thought that would happen. And there was only one reason it was happening now. Not because he'd suddenly realised what a fool he'd been all this time, but because she looked different. But Fusani had noticed her right away, hadn't he? Was it her imagination, or had he volunteered to give her mouth-to-mouth after her experience in the tomb? And wasn't that before she changed? And even then, her dad wouldn't let him near her lips. What was up with that?

It took a while before it occurred to her that Chris had been talking to her and she hadn't been listening.

"Huh?"

"I said I have practice, but if you need a ride later..."

"Thanks," she replied, "I've already got one."

Chris was visibly confused by her rejection. "Oh. Okay."

She left him standing on the steps, staring after her.

"So how was your first day?" Bruce asked as he climbed out of the car.

"It didn't totally suck," she answered.

"Well, I got you a little present."

Probably it wasn't any gift of prophecy from Isis, but Alex seemed to know before her father even opened the passenger door what the present would turn out to be.

"Oh my Goddess!"

"You'll be my tour guide, right, Alex?" That smile. That smile.

She dropped her books and threw her arms around Fusani.

"What are you doing here?" she asked, rocking her from side to side with the force of her hug.

"School doesn't start for another month in Cairo," he explained.

Alex pulled back, expecting her dad to intervene at any second, bellowing, "Not with my daughter you don't, young man!"

But Bruce was still over by the car. And when she caught his eye, he looked away, contemplating the school's architecture.

Fusani was still smiling. She smiled back, and she was no longer a superhero with the powers of an Egyptian Goddess; she was a seventeen year-old, still innocent, frightened and joyful at the same time, and ready for her first kiss.

As her lips touched his, she thought: Totally worth it.

THE END

About the Author

Matthew J Elliott is a writer and radio dramatist living in the United Kingdom.

He is the author of *Sherlock Holmes on the Air*, and has contributed stories to the collections *Curious Incidents 2*, *The Game's Afoot* and *Gaslight Grimoire*. His story *Art in the Blood* can be found in *The Mammoth Book of Best British Mysteries 8*. Matthew is the editor of *The Whisperer in Darkness*, *The Horror in the Museum* and *The Haunter of the Dark* by H P Lovecraft, *The Right Hand of Doom* and *The Haunter of the Ring* by Robert E Howard, and *A Charlie Chan Omnibus* by Earl Derr Biggers. His articles, fiction and reviews have appeared in the magazines *SHERLOCK*, *Total DVD* and *Scarlet Street*.

For the radio, he has scripted episodes of *The Twilight Zone*, *Fangoria's Dreadtime Stories*, *Wrath of the Titans*, *Vincent Price Presents*, *The Further Adventures of Sherlock Holmes*, *The Classic Adventures of Sherlock Holmes*, *Raffles the Gentleman Thief*, *The Father Brown Mysteries*, *Kincaid the Strangeseeker*, *The Adventures of Harry Nile*, *The Perry Mason Radio Dramas*, *Jeeves and Wooster*, *Masters of Mystery* and the Audie Award-nominated *New Adventures of Mickey Spillane's Mike Hammer*. He is the creator of *The Hilary Caine Mysteries*, which first aired in 2005. His stage play *An Evening With Jeeves & Wooster* was performed at the Palace Theatre, Grapevine, Texas in 2007.

Matthew works with the makers of cult sci-fi comedy *Mystery Science Theater 3000* on their RiffTrax website, writing and recording humorous commentaries for hit movies. *The Legend of Isis* is his first novel.

DORIAN GRAY

High school junior Dorian Gray lives a life of total excess. But when he receives his great-grandfather's portrait and journal, Dorian finds himself in the middle of the ultimate battle of good vs. evil. Now Dorian must put all his fears aside and figure out whom he can really trust.

ISBN: 978-1-911243-63-2

ALSO AVAILABLE FROM MARKOSIA

SINBAD: ROGUE OF MARS

A prophecy foretells of a stranger from distant lands who will vanquish the false king. Eight years after the assassination of King Dadgar, his vile nephew, Adhkar, has usurped his throne and enslaved the Azurian people, igniting a violent civil war. Having sailed the seven seas, exploring unknown lands, fighting countless monsters and battling evil wizards, could Sinbad be the stranger of the prophecy, or will he merely be a pawn in Adhkar's bloody game?

ISBN: 978-1-911243-63-2

ALSO AVAILABLE FROM MARKOSIA

WORDS ON A WALL

Monsters, cryogenics, relationships, religion, war, dragons, cannibalism, angels, demons, space exploration, aliens, beans, eyes, traffic cones, gods, Chicago, pot plants, robots, a dive bar on Mars, goblins, heart break, July, cake, bees, geese, peacock flavour crisps and time travel are just some of the things you'll find in this eclectic collection of flash fiction and poetry. At times incredibly dark and deeply personal but often very, very silly.

ISBN: 978-1-911243-63-2

www.ingramcontent.com/pod-product-compliance
Lightning Source LLC
Chambersburg PA
CBHW070925180626
46817CB00003B/1195